# Dark
## GUARDIAN

# Dark Guardian

Grace Halfpenny has devoted her entire life to her career as a social worker. Always playing by the rules. Always going all in. Falling in love is the last thing Grace had time for.

Eugene "Judge" Grant is the president of the Black Hoods MC. A hardass son of a bitch, thanks to the scars of his past. Love is the last thing Judge believed in.

Two people on two very different paths. Until...

Two kids, orphaned and alone with a past that mirrored Judges' own, come along, not only needing him, but Grace too.

And when the kids' dark past comes looking for them, Grace and Judge must put their differences aside in order to save them.

To moonshine for getting us through the first leg of the pandemic.

Tequila don't let us down for the second.

## Grace

"YOU DON'T UNDERSTAND, ma'am. I've filled out every single sheet of paperwork this office has asked me to provide. Why won't you release the information to me?" the man sitting on the other side of my desk pleads, his story the same as so many others.

And *ma'am?* Really? Am I so old now that a man, no more than ten years my junior, thinks of me as *ma'am?* Is forty the new fifty? I don't dare think of what my clients will call me when I hit that milestone. *Granny? Old Bitty?* The thought makes me shudder.

"Mr. Jackson, I'm sorry, but my hands are tied. There are rules we have to follow." I straighten in my chair. "You need to wait for your court date. That's all there is to it. Your attorney should have informed you of that."

"I'm tired of waiting. I tried to do this without the

courts. I submitted my DNA to some online database for kids looking for family and got nothing. This my only option, and you won't give me what I came for?"

"I'm sorry," I force out, trying to keep my voice calm. "I know you've been looking for your parents for a long time, but there's only so much I can do."

I notice his hands balling into fists on top of my desk. He's angry. Furious, actually, but it changes nothing. He'd have more luck pulling a white rabbit out of a magic hat than getting the answers he so desperately wants from me. Answers I don't have authority or permission to share.

"You don't want to help me," he hisses through clenched teeth. "I have a *right* to know."

"Whether it's your right or not, I can't help you without a court order to release the information. The records were sealed. I can't unseal them without approval."

"This is bullshit!" His eyes, pleading with my compassionate side just moments ago, now flash with fury. I myself have questioned over the last few years if compassion still exists after seeing so many families torn apart in some form or another. This place hardens even the gentlest of people. Social work is not for the faint of heart, and boy, have I learned that the hard way.

"Please, watch your language. This is a place of busi-

2

ness," I admonish him quietly. He goes to argue with me, but I quickly raise my hand to cut off his tirade. "As I explained to you the last time you scheduled an appointment with my office, this is in the court's hands. Wait for your court date, then we'll proceed from there."

"All I've done is wait."

"I understand that. Believe me, I do. But there's nothing more I can do. It's in the hands of the judge. Your attorney should have notified you of that."

"My attorney assured me this would be an easy process, though it's been far from it. Is there anyone else I can speak to?"

"You can take this up with the supervisor, but he's not going to bend the rules for you, either. Stay the course and wait until your court date."

Defeated, he slides his hands off the desk and slumps back into his chair. If I had the ability to help him with his query, I'd remove the file from the locked records room and hand it over without batting an eye, but I have to follow the rules set forth by the courts or risk losing my job, which is something I cannot do. Jeopardizing it for one person affects the dozens of children in the case files scattered across my desk. Our department has always been understaffed, and with opioid use on the rise, more and more children are becoming wards of the state, so we're stretching ourselves even thinner. It's a dangerous game of chance when a child's life is at stake in an abusive home.

In Mr. Jackson's case, the names of his birth parents don't fall into the "emergency" category. He's an adult. If he were a child, it would be a different story, but he's not. There's nothing I can do except offer my sympathy and pray it will be enough until the court makes a decision.

He's silent, but I can see the wheels turning in his head. He wants to beg me, offer me something that could tempt me into breaking the rules, but it's not going to work. He knows that from the last time he tried it.

"Is there anything else I can help you with today?"

His eyes harden, turning cold, dark. "No." Getting to his feet, he spins on one foot and storms out of my office.

I count to ten before I allow myself to sigh in relief. Days like today are never easy. Every person who walks through the doors of our office thinks that if they press hard enough, we'll cave, giving them all the answers to cheat the system. That's not how it works. I'm bound by the governance of the State of Texas, and I won't bypass the laws in place to protect my clients' information.

Hearing a knock at the door, I peer up to find Cindy, one of the other social workers in my branch, dressed in a pink tailored business suit, her gray curls springing off the side of her head in multiple directions.

"How'd court go?" I inquire. The case she'd been

assigned to has been particularly difficult these past few weeks, with four young souls separated into different foster homes while their grandmother fought for custody.

"Judge ruled against the grandmother." Cindy's eyes soften as a single tear glides down her cheek, her reaction mirroring my own. No one in our line of work is impervious to the painful things we so often see.

"That's too bad."

The children's elderly grandmother stepped up the second her wayward son had been arrested for a drug charge, but she lives in an assisted living community that doesn't allow children. I had a feeling the court would rule against her, being that she had no means of finding alternative housing, as well as her medical ailments. It's one of the few parts of this job that still bothers me after all these years, seeing the heartbreak of families being torn apart under circumstances such as this. As hard as they try, it's just not enough in the eyes of the court of law.

"So, how was your meeting with Mr. Jackson? I saw him as I was coming back from the court. He looked... pleasant," she asks with a smirk. *Pleasant.* Not the exact term I would use to describe him. A thorn in my side would be more apt.

"He's not happy that I couldn't push through his request prior to the court date."

"I wish they would realize our power is limited. We're caseworkers, not magicians. We can't just wave a magic wand and *poof!* The judge makes a ruling in their favor."

The image makes me laugh. No wand on Earth would make a judge work any faster. And with some of the judges in our county, I'd rather use the wand to dismiss them than summon them like the devils they are, especially the one assigned to Mr. Jackson's case. Judge McAdams is a stubborn man when it comes to child service cases. His track record is far from great. I can count on one hand the number of times he's ruled in the loving parent's favor.

"Me too, Cindy, but it's easier to berate the messenger, it seems."

Looking at her watch, she smiles. "Almost quitting time. Got any big plans this weekend?"

*Plans? Me?* You'd think after six years of working together, Cindy would know me better than that. My work comes first. I can't just switch it off when I walk out the door like everyone else. The children stay with me every waking moment of the day, and even when I close my eyes. These kids need me. I can't let my hair down, so to speak, because the second I do, something will happen, and I won't be there in time to protect them.

"The usual. You?"

"My husband and I are heading to the Gulf for a weekend getaway."

"Must be nice," I mutter under my breath, but she thankfully doesn't catch it, or doesn't acknowledge it. It's been at least ten years since my last vacation. Maybe even longer than that. I've lost more paid vacation time for not using it than I've probably used, but there's no point in taking a trip if it's just me. I can be alone in my own house for far cheaper.

"I hope you both enjoy your time away. Do you need me to cover anything for you?"

"No, but I appreciate you asking. I worked late the last few nights so everything was caught up before I left. My court date today was the last thing on my to-do list."

"Well, if anything comes up——."

"I know, you'll cover it," she interjects. "But I wish you'd take some time off for yourself. Between this and all your volunteer work, you deserve it."

"I appreciate that, but you know I can't."

"One of these days, I'm going to convince you to do it."

"You always say that, and it never works."

"One day, it will." Winking, she pats the folders resting on her arm. "I better get these files into the system. Mark will kill me if I work late tonight. You have a wonderful weekend."

"You, too."

Spinning on her heels, she disappears, leaving me to finish up a few more things before the alarm on my phone goes off. Shit, it's already six. If I don't hurry, I'll be late for my date with Greg. The last time I was late, he was an absolute bear. Not that his mood is ever really cheerful.

Grabbing my things, I shut off the remaining lights in the office and lock the door behind me, praying that traffic will be light as I make my way to the car.

## Judge

"COME ON, GUYS!" I call up the stairs for the third time. "You're gonna be late for your first day!" I never thought I'd ever say those words, but here I am, instant father to two very traumatized kids.

Kevin comes thumping down the steps first, pulling his shirt over his head. "Sorry," he mumbles, brushing past me and plopping his ass down into a kitchen chair. "Didn't sleep so good last night."

I watch him for a moment. "What's going on, son?"

Shrugging, he peers at the empty plate in front of him. "Just nervous, I guess."

Poor fucking kid. He'd been through more shit at sixteen than most grown men I know, and he's still here, powering on, taking care of his sister, and trying to give them both a good life. His shit past will make him into a good father someday.

"Where's Nat?"

Kevin worries his lower lip between his teeth. "Uh, she's coming. She was just trying to look her best, I think." She and Lindsey had picked out her outfit over a week ago. I know girls can be finicky about their clothes, but as many bags as the two of them brought into the house from the mall, she has more than enough options. My credit card is proof of that.

I sigh. Kevin's a shit liar.

"Eat," I order, pointing at the plates in the center of the table piled high with scrambled eggs, toast, and sausages. I admit, I went overboard, but both kids are skin and bones, and I'll be damned if I send them off to their first day at a new school on an empty stomach.

Leaving Kevin to his breakfast, I take the stairs two at a time, glancing at the clock on my phone as I get near the top. *Shit.*

"Nat, honey, ya gotta hurry. We need to leave in a few minutes."

"Coming." The bathroom door at the end of the hall muffles her reply, but not enough that I can't hear the sadness in her voice.

I move toward the door and tap it a few times with my knuckle. "Everything okay in there, kiddo?"

I hear her sniff. "Um, yeah. I just…"

"You just what, Nat? What's going on?" I grip the knob and twist it gently, when what I really want to do is rip the whole damn thing off its hinges. "Open this door."

Hearing her quiet sobs, I take in a deep breath and blow it out slowly, preparing myself for the worst. I listen as her hand rests on the knob, and without a word, she pulls the door open.

Her face is red, her eyes puffy and swollen. Her hair is in some sort of a twist at the side of her head, but even I know that's not right.

"I just can't get my hair right," she cries, her sobs now chest-wracking gasps.

She looks so tiny for a twelve-year-old. The kids at her new school are going to tower over her, and I hate the idea of leaving her there. She's so broken, so soft-hearted. Maybe she's not ready. I know Lindsey says to try, that she needs to interact with her peers and rediscover what it's like to be a normal kid, but she's not a normal fucking kid. Not after what she's been through.

"Can you braid hair, Mr. Judge?"

*Mr. Judge.* I don't know how many times I've told her to call me plain Judge, or even by my actual name, but she continues to call me Mr. Judge. And I'm not gonna lie, I kinda like it. It's special, something between just the two of us. "I can't say I do, shug. I've never had much of a reason to learn."

Sighing, she pulls the elastic band from her hair. I watch, my heart cracking a little more as she stares at her own reflection in the mirror and runs a brush through her locks. "I guess down is good enough," she whispers.

The sadness in her voice pisses me off, but not at her. Never at her. I'm pissed at her pervert uncle, the man who did this to her. I'm pissed at the legal system that allowed it to happen. I'm pissed at all the men who have ever looked upon this child with anything other than fatherly affection. And most of all, I'm pissed I never learned how to fucking braid hair.

She places the brush down on the counter and turns to me, her lips pushed up into a smile that isn't fooling anyone. "Ready."

"Maybe you shouldn't go to school today." I hate the thought of dropping her off when I know she's struggling.

Natalie's eyes soften as she peers up at me. "I'm okay. Promise."

I want to believe her. I think she even wants to believe it herself. She's trying to put on a brave face, but maybe Lindsey is wrong about this. Maybe it's too soon to force her back to school.

"Hey, Nat, come eat." Kevin stands at the top of the

stairs, motioning for his sister to get her ass in gear. "We gotta leave in five minutes, and I don't want to be late."

Without another word, she pushes past me and descends the stairs behind her brother. I watch their backs as they go, marveling at the strength they've both shown since coming to live with me. But the one thing they don't understand yet is, they don't have to be strong. Not anymore. I'm strong enough for all three of us.

And if anyone upsets either of them today, I'll show that strength when I rip some fucking heads off.

Kevin and I both watch as she pushes her food around on her plate, only nibbling on a piece of toast until I announce that it's time to leave.

The kids pile into my pickup truck without a word. A few minutes later, we're standing out front of their school. They look so damn lost in the sea of teenagers as they stare up at the large building, their backpacks hanging from their shoulders.

"You guys good?"

Both kids turn toward me, and even though their faces say they're ready, their eyes scream they're not. "Ready," Kevin says, taking his sister's hand. "We got this, Gene. Promise."

And he does. I can tell by the determined set of his jaw. I just wish his sister looked as confident.

"Shug, what about you?"

Natalie straightens her shoulders. "I'll be okay, Mr. Judge. You don't have to worry about us."

A lump forms in my throat as she speaks, and I can't tell if it's because of my own fear for her, or if it's because she never ceases to amaze me. Maybe it's both. Who fucking knows? "You got your phones. Call me if you need me, for anything, okay?"

They both nod in unison.

"I mean it. I can be here in less than five minutes. Just say the word."

Natalie's hand lands on my arm, her touch as light as a butterfly. "We're gonna be okay."

Kevin chuckles. "It's school, man, not prison. Go do your thing. We'll see you after."

"You want me to walk you in?"

Finally, Natalie giggles and shoves at my arm playfully, attempting to move me toward my truck. "Go! We're fine."

I allow her to move me away and laugh with her, the lump in my throat loosening just a little. "All right, all right, I'm going. Have a great first day, guys."

As I pull away from the school, I catch a group of women standing near the entrance with their kids in tow, every single one of them smiling when I creep by.

Smirking, I wave. "Morning, ladies." Several of them drag their kids into the building, while the rest stare back with hungry looks on their faces. Gotta love moms. Maybe this school thing won't be so bad.

Chapter 3

Grace

THE COLDEST PAIR of green eyes stare at me from across the table.

"You're late," Greg growls, puffing out his chest as he looks down at his watch. His beard is more unruly than usual, sticking out in every direction. He's also in dire need of a haircut.

"For goodness' sake, I'm three minutes late." I settle into the chair across from him and set my purse down beside me in the booth. "It's not like I missed the whole darn thing."

"Still late. I don't have all day to wait on you."

He's lying, of course. Greg has all the time in the world. Even if he doesn't want to admit it, he likes our standing Friday night card games at the soup kitchen. Greg had stumbled into my life after he'd helped scare off two teenagers trying to steal my purse when I was walking to my car. And here I am, three years later, still trying to repay him for his bravery, of which is against his will.

"I'm sorry, but I brought you something that might cheer you up."

His brow arches in interest. Slipping my hand into my bag, I pull out a wrapped Whataburger. His entire attitude changes when I set it on the table and slide it over. Snatching it up, he devours the burger in four bites.

"Better?" I laugh when he runs his weathered thumb across his lips before sucking it into his mouth.

"Would've been better if you'd gotten me two of them."

I slip the second burger from my purse and hand it to him, watching his perpetual frown slip into the tiniest smile. Stuffing it into his worn Army jacket pocket, he pats it in satisfaction.

"I'll forgive you this time, but don't be late again."

I roll my eyes. He'll never admit it, but he enjoys our Friday nights together, even if I am late more often than not. I just wish I could visit with him more, but my case-load prevents it.

"How have things been this week?" I ask, trying to make small talk while he's still in a good mood.

"Weather's been shit. Too hot." It has been hot,

topping in the upper nineties for the past three weeks. I can barely stand it, so I have no doubt it's been awful in his tent a few blocks away. The place he wouldn't have to live in if he'd just take me up on my offer.

"There's air conditioning at the VA."

"I ain't goin' to no VA. Those bastards sent me to Nam, and they'll try to send me back."

"The war has been over since 1973," I chuckle. "I'm pretty sure at 72, you don't meet the age requirement for active duty."

"Doesn't mean they won't try."

It's the same argument we have every week. I offer to get him off the streets, and he fires back nonsense at me. It's the definition of insanity, but it won't stop me from trying. After finally getting him to open up to me last year, I was able to verify his veteran status, and even had a caseworker set up for him. But he won't go. It's frustrating, to say the least.

"They aren't going to send you back, Greg. They just want to help you get medical care and give you a safe place to live."

"I said no, didn't I? N-O. Even spelled it for ya."

"You did, but you earned this with your service."

He crosses his arms over his chest, attempting to look intimidating. "They didn't do shit for me when I lost my job, my house, or my life. Why should I trust them to house and feed me?"

I stifle a sigh. He has to be the stubbornest man on the planet. He could have a warm bed to sleep in and round-the-clock medical care, but he won't budge. When he left the Army, things were in a constant state of flux for benefits and support. How he got lost in the shuffle, I'll never know, but after a few calls and a push from a friend higher up in the food chain, I'd secured him a spot at the local VAs assisted living facility. All he had to do was show up.

"Consider it," I urge.

"No," he fires back. "Are we playing, or do you plan to sit there all night, gabbing and clucking at me like ladies at a beauty parlor?" Greg has always been blunt and to the point since the day we met. If he's ready to move on, you can either comply, or he'll just get up and leave. There is no middle ground with him.

"Fine. But this conversation isn't over. Poker or Gin Rummy?"

Pulling out a worn deck of cards from his other jacket pocket, he opens the box and shuffles the deck, his fingers nimble for his age. Without so much as another word, he deals out a hand and lays the cards down in front of me.

"Poker. And the bet is more of those burgers."

Greg cracks the first smile of the night. And true to his word, he earns himself at least a dozen burgers over the course of our playing time. I'm not what you would call a card shark, but I'm decent. Greg, however, is a pro. If I hadn't called off the last game when I did, I'd be buying stock in Whataburger to pay off my debt to him.

"Giving up easy today, kid?" he teases.

I motion to the setting sun outside the booth's window and say, "It's getting late."

"Past your curfew, eh?"

"I don't have a curfew," I mumble back.

"Neither do I, so why the rush? I need to earn some more burgers before you start trying to beat me."

"It's been a long week," I lie. Greg is still a capable guy, but I'd rather that both of us weren't out on the streets this late at night.

Nodding, he gathers up the cards and pops the deck back into his pocket before we shove out of the booth.

"Don't forget what you owe me, Grace. Extra cheese, and maybe some fries."

I laugh at his demands. He knows I'll get him whatever he wants, and that's how our relationship has been since he rescued me. He may grumble about being able to take care of himself, but if he really needs it, he'll give in soon enough. Blankets, coats, and gift cards, or cash for food, are just drops in the bucket to what I'd like to do for him. I just wish he'd be more open about the VA. But hopefully, I can convince him to go there soon.

"I won't forget."

"Don't be late."

"I guess we'll see what happens," I throw back over my shoulder. "Maybe I'll have a date next Friday night."

"Yeah, me," he scoffs. "But if you do find yourself a man, he better come with you. I'm going to have some questions for him."

Yeah, right. There has never been a man in my life, and I doubt there ever will be. No one wants to be involved with a workaholic who can never make plans.

Chuckling, I shake my head. "See you next week."

He follows closely behind me until I reach my car and unlock the door. Satisfied that I'm safe, he turns, heading toward his tent home, but stops and waits until I'm inside my car. The engine of my Volvo starts up on the first turn of the ignition, and with a wave, I pull out of my parking spot. Standing on the corner, he watches until I disappear around the corner.

Most nights, I'd listen to music during my drive, but silence is more fitting for my current mood. The banter between Greg and me as we played earlier runs through my thoughts instead.

How many other veterans like him are on the streets right now because they fell through the cracks?

It breaks my heart to know these men and women put their lives on the line to protect our country, and we've failed them so badly. Greg is one of the luckier ones since our chance meeting, but a part of me wants to advocate more for those like him. Between my own work, and volunteering at Greg's shelter throughout the week to help support the attached soup kitchens serving line, my plate is already full. Yet, there has to be some way I can help them. I just have to find it.

My older apartment complex comes into view within ten minutes of leaving the shelter. The old brick contrasts against the new luxury apartments that continue to pop up in the historical district of Austin. Where families used to live in beautiful historic homes, younger couples and singles now dot the sidewalks, dressed in fancy clothes, carrying their coffee in one hand and their phones in the other.

As I park my car in my designated spot next to the entrance of my building, two younger women in skirts that leave zero to the imagination, and heels high enough to reach Heaven's gates, trot by me toward a waiting Prius with a ride share logo in the back window a block away, their giggles echoing off the surrounding buildings.

"I miss the old neighborhood," I murmur under my breath, walking up the stairs to the front entrance. My apartment is on the first floor of the building near the back. With most of my neighbors nearing Greg's age, it's quiet at night, which I love. Work is far from quiet, and the silence at home in the evenings is almost therapeutic.

Unlocking my door, I step inside and flick on the light switch to my left, flooding the apartment in a soft, warm glow. The small space I call home, with such historic charm, has exposed brick walls and original hardwood floors. They were the biggest draw when this apartment came up for sale in this building. And the close commute to work was a bonus.

Setting my keys and purse down on the entryway table, I utter, "Home sweet home." Home sweet, lonely home is more like it. I'd considered over the years getting a pet, but it wouldn't be fair to them with the hours I keep.

I head toward the kitchen when I catch my reflection in the mirror above the table. My dark hair lays in loose waves on either side of my round face, with little wisps of gray baby hairs dotting my hairline near my ears. My gray eyes behind my wire-frame glasses showcase my extreme exhaustion.

Sighing, I jump when my cell phone rings from inside my purse.

Retrieving it quickly, I answer, "Grace Halfpenny."

"Hey, Grace," the voice of my supervisor, Eric, comes through the line. "I'm sorry to call so late."

"It's okay. Is something wrong?" Please say no. I just got home and haven't even taken off my shoes.

"Austin PD requested crisis prevention for a removal. Parent OD'd in the car outside of a Denny's. I wouldn't normally ask, but with Cindy out of the office..." he trails off.

"It's fine. What's the address?"

Rattling it off, he apologizes again before hanging up. Without even a second thought, I gather my things, take a deep breath, and step back out into the night's air. No rest for the weary, right?

## Judge

"I DON'T HAVE THAT," I repeat, walking away from the others to gain a little privacy. I've been on the phone with the school's secretary for almost ten minutes now, having this same conversation over and over again. The same one I'd had when I went to register them a few days before school started.

"Sir, we need to have the children's birth certificates, transcriptions from their previous school, and vaccination records for their files. Surely you have them somewhere."

Feeling my eye twitch, I clench the phone in my hand. I know she's just doing her job, but how many ways can I say it? "Look, I don't have them. I'll work on getting replacements for your files, but those kids need to stay in school."

"Of course." From the sounds of it, she's just as

pissed off as I am. "I can let it go for *now,* as legally, we can't keep them from enrolling in school," she snaps, emphasizing the last word to reinforce the idea that this isn't the end of it. "But please, keep me informed on where you're at with attaining those documents."

"Will do," I growl, but the phone disconnects before I finish, making it painfully obvious I've been dismissed. *Stupid bitch.*

Before I have time to stew over being hung up on, my phone rings. With a sigh that's supposed to be calming, I look down at the screen. *Mom* is calling.

"What do you want, asshole?" I greet, bringing the phone back up to my ear.

Mom chuckles on the other end. "Fuck you too, prick. Is that any way to talk to your buddy after not speaking for three months?"

I grin. "Pretty sure it's not my fault. Your phone works just as well as mine does."

Mom groans on the other end. "I wasn't exactly on vacation here, Judge."

"I know, I asked you to go there." My smile fades. "You good, brother?"

"I'm coming home, man. I've done all I can do here, and shit with Marie is hitting the fucking fan. I gotta sort out my own life before I can do much more for this club."

I lean my ass against a nearby picnic table and stare down at the ground. "You got an escort?"

"Yeah. V is heading back with me. Thinking he might stick around a while."

"Good. Get your ass home, brother. The club needs their VP back in one piece."

"Their VP needs his old lady to stop being such a fuckin' psycho."

I chuckle, knowing that Mom loves Marie's psychotic side almost as much as her fancy new tits. "See you soon."

Disconnecting the call, I shove my phone back into my pocket. Mom and I have been around since the beginning of the Black Hoods MC. We've seen and done a lot of shit together. He's been gone, dealing with an upheaval in the SoCal chapter, but I wasn't lying when I said we needed our VP back.

Not only does Mom fill that role in our club, but his name is Mom for a reason. These guys look up to him. He takes care of them, offers advice, and bakes fucking pies, of all things. He's a weird fucker, but he's ours.

And even if the club didn't need him, I do. Becoming an instant dad hasn't been easy, and who better to offer me parenting advice than the man who has a pack of burly, grown-ass bikers calling him Mom?

A car pulls into the parking lot, and Karma motions for me to get my ass in gear.

Moving toward the others, I watch as Sharon Palmer pulls up to the front of the garage and gets out of her car. Sharon is an old friend. We'd gone to high school together, and her old man had been a good friend to the Black Hoods before he died. She's also the real estate agent listed on this particular garage.

"Hello, boys," she purrs, sliding her sunglasses up on top of her head while flashing us all an easy smile. The woman has balls of steel. Not too many people would be comfortable pulling up to a parking lot filled with Black Hoods, especially not good-looking women driving a fancy Tesla.

"How you doin', darlin'?" I ask, stepping forward and holding out a hand to her.

"Can't complain." Grasping my hand in hers, she gives it a firm shake, not once losing her smile. "But only 'cause complaining is against company policy." Turning to the others, she throws out her arms. "So, I hear you boys are in the market for a new garage?"

"Don't think there are many of those kickin' around here, are there?" Karma drawls.

"Just this one," she replies, pointing at the building behind us. "Let's go take a look around." We all follow as she walks toward the front door and unlocks three different deadbolts. "What kind of business are you hoping to run here? Body shop? Maybe a custom motorcycle garage?"

I look around the reception area of the old garage. It needs some TLC, for sure, but it definitely has the potential to be exactly what we'd all been hoping for.

"Neither," I respond. "This town needs a basic garage. Just somewhere to go for a tune-up, or an oil change. Find out what the squeal from under the hood is coming from without paying an arm and a leg for shit parts."

"Well, this place would be good for that." She opens the door to the garage bay. "There are six bays here, each of them with fully operational lifts and power doors. And right through here,"—she enters another door at the back —"is a bathroom, a small kitchenette, a furnace room with space for storage, and an office. The property extends all the way to the corner if you'd want to expand the structure in the future. Perfect for the right buyer who has an eye for a deal and a steady hand for renovations."

She stands back as each of us moves around, looking into the different rooms, assessing the potential of making this a lucrative business for our club.

I try to focus and keep my mind on this piece of club business, but all I can think about are the kids. I wonder how they're doing, and if that bitch in the office gave them a hard time about not having birth certificates.

"Everything okay, boss?"

Hashtag's voice snaps me out of my thoughts, but also gives me an idea. "Not really," I admit. "Hash, you think you can hack into the school computer system?"

He frowns. "Do I ask why?"

I explain the missing paperwork and my lack of proof for being a legal guardian to Kevin and Natalie.

"Shouldn't be too hard. I'll work on it as soon as we finish up here."

"Well," Sharon says, approaching the two of us with a smile. "What do you think?"

I glance over at Karma, who nods his approval, and say, "Guess we're makin' an offer."

"I'll draw up the paperwork. How would you like to pay if they accept it?"

"Cash, sugar. Cold, hard cash."

Chapter 5

Grace

MY PHONE RINGS the second I sit down at my desk.

"Grace Halfpenny."

"Hi, Grace, it's Lisa in the call center. How are you?" she chirps cheerfully. How someone can be that happy at seven in the morning on a Monday is beyond me, but I don't think I've ever seen Lisa crack a frown once since I've known her. She's just one of those cheery people.

"Fine, thank you. How can I help you?"

"We just received a call on the anonymous tip line regarding two children at the Lake Travis School District."

Looking for a pad of paper and a pen, I jot down the details as she rattles them off.

"Caller said two kids, a boy and a girl, were enrolled at Lake Travis Secondary School on the first day without any paperwork to prove guardianship. No birth certificates, transcripts from their old school, or shot records."

"Odd," I comment.

"The caller stated they got a bad feeling from the man with them and noted he was a bit old to have kids of that age." Being a later in life parent isn't as uncommon as it used to be, but it's interesting that the caller mentioned it.

Something in this caller's description sets off a wave of uneasiness inside of me. Who is he? And why doesn't he have the paperwork to prove these kids are under his care?

I write this on the notepad and underline it.

"Did the caller provide their names? Address? Descriptions?"

"Kevin and Natalie Tucker. They were registered as siblings."

"Did the caller mention anything else?"

"That was the gist of it. They didn't stay on long enough for the call center to ask anything else."

"Thank you for bringing this to my attention, Lisa. I appreciate it."

She hangs up, and I fire off an email to my supervisor to alert him to the call.

Flipping open my computer, I search for the school contact information. Speaking to these kids as soon as possible is essential, but according to the school website, the central office won't be open for a few more hours. Until then, I have to bide my time, looking through our old records for a possible connection just to be sure.

Switching to our internal database, I type in their names, and with a stroke of the enter key, two case numbers with those names associated pop up.

I start with the oldest record. Clicking on the date, it pulls up a case file with two images across the top. The boy has dark hair and dark eyes, and the nearly identical little girl with blue eyes is clutching a teddy bear to her chest. My heart sinks the longer I take in the images on the screen. What had happened to them to make their faces so full of fear and sadness?

*Could these be the same kids?* Without seeing them in person, I have no way to be sure. I send the images to my printer to add to my file.

Anger stirs inside me when I scroll further down into the history of the case. Their mother was arrested for prostitution, and they placed the kids into foster care. Custody was returned to the mother a year later.

The last file is almost identical. Mother loses custody after a second arrest for prostitution, forcing the kids back into foster care a second time. However, they were separated after the foster family requested an alternative home when the kids had attempted to run away together. The little girl's foster family went so far as to file a petition for adoption, but the judge denied it. The boy was another story. He bounced around to several other foster homes until their mother was granted her rights back a second time, after eighteen months.

Why would the courts side with this woman and not with so many others who had worked to clean up their life? Why did she deserve her kids more than someone who had gotten their life back on track? The logical answer would be that she didn't, but the decision was clear in black and white on the screen in front of me. The courts said she did. If these kids are the same as my new case, I can only imagine what level of hell they've been through over the years.

Trying to put that notion out of my mind and focus on the kids, I work a few more hours until Eric walks into my office and settles into one of the chairs across from my desk. "Good morning, Grace."

"Eric," I return.

"Got your email. What have you found so far?" I turn my computer screen to show him the two case files I had found in the system. Reading them, he shakes his head. "I remember this case. One of your predecessors, I believe. The mother was a real piece of work. The whole office was shocked when they gave her her rights back. Happens far too often in cases like this."

"I'd be inclined to agree with you, sir."

"Where are you at with the school?"

"Just waiting for them to open." Shifting my eyes to the clock on my computer screen, I see it's twenty past nine. I quickly reach for my phone as Eric pushes himself out of the chair.

"Keep me posted," he remarks over his shoulder as he leaves me to the call.

"Here goes nothing," I mutter as I dial the number I'd found on Google for the school. Someone picks up almost immediately.

"Lake Travis Secondary School," a cheerful voice answers.

"Yes, my name is Grace Halfpenny, and I'm a caseworker with the Texas Department of Family and Protective Services. I'm calling because our office has been made aware of a situation involving two students, a boy and a girl who were enrolled into your school last week." Pulling my notepad out from underneath a stack of papers, I place it in front of me. "Kevin and Natalie Tucker."

"Ma'am, I'm sorry, but I can't release any information about our students. It's against policy."

"Maybe you didn't hear me. I'm calling from—"

"It doesn't change the answer," she fires back.

I stifle my frustration as I try to remain professional. "Is there someone else I can speak with? A principal or superintendent, perhaps?" She remains silent, so I continue. "I understand you may not get calls like this all that often, but I'm investigating a report we received about two students enrolled in your school. You can either allow me to speak to someone who can verify the information I require, or I'll request law enforcement to collect it for me." My voice wavers as my professionalism cracks.

"Can you hold just a second?"

"Sure." The phone line clicks over to soft jazz music in the background. It plays for a few minutes before the line clicks back over.

A new voice comes onto the line. "Miss Halfpenny? My name is Melanie Pyle, and I'm the superintendent for the school. My secretary, a new hire, has informed me of your request. How can we help you?"

I repeat my earlier request.

"Yes, of course," she answers matter-of-factly. "Can I please have the names of the students?"

"Kevin and Natalie Tucker."

"Ah, yes. The principal of their school contacted me about the peculiarities of their enrollment. I assume that's the reason for your call?"

"That's correct. I'd like to meet with them to conduct my investigation. Will that be a problem?"

"Let me check our attendance roll." I hear the clicks

of a keyboard in the background as she types. "It looks like we have marked Natalie absent today. Let me pull up the notes." Her keyboard clicks a few more times before she sighs. "It says illness."

"And Kevin?"

"He's also marked as absent for illness. Unfortunately, there's been a case of the first week flu, as we like to call it, hitting several of our grades. We have twenty percent of our student body out today."

"I see." If they aren't there, I can't identify or match them with the previous cases. I only have one choice. I have to wait for them to come back to school and try to track down their whereabouts in the meantime. "Speaking to them both is of the utmost priority right now."

This isn't how I envisioned this going. Pushing my glasses up, I pinch the bridge of my nose and ask another question. "Did the man who registered them provide a place of residence? An address or phone number? Any means to contact them?"

"Unfortunately, that information is still being entered our system. We've had an influx of new students this year, and we're behind. I can reach out to our IT department and ask them to expedite their information upload."

"That would be helpful. I'd appreciate a copy being sent to my office, and request that I be notified when they return to class. I must stress, Ms. Pyle, that these children might be in danger, and any second we waste could come with dire consequences for them."

"I understand. If you give me your number and email address, I'll get what information we have to you as soon as possible."

I rattle off my number, and the second she hangs up, I cup my face in my hands.

It can never be easy, can it?

## Judge

"KNOCK-KNOCK," Lindsey calls from the front door. My niece knows full well she never has to knock before entering this house. I raised her here from the time she was twelve years old. My home is her home, even if she doesn't actually live here anymore.

And besides, I've been waiting for her.

"In the kitchen," I call out, trying to keep my voice calm, even as the panic threatens to claw its way up my throat and out of my mouth.

I force a smile for Kevin, who looks as worried as I feel.

"You're home too?" Lindsey asks him as she bustles into the room.

"Something's wrong with Nat," he replies.

Lindsey nods, but doesn't comment any further on the matter. Smart girl.

Lindsey is in the final year of her PhD program at the local university. When she's finished, she'll be a fully licensed psychiatrist. But there's a pretty good chance she'll push it even further and move on in the program to specialize specifically in child psychiatry. I'm proud as hell of her, but I never thought her expertise would come in as handy as it does right now.

"She's locked herself in the bathroom and she won't come out," I explain. "She woke up fine, went in there to get ready for school, then let out this god-awful scream. I can hear her crying in there, but when I threatened to break down the door, she begged me to just leave her alone."

"And a little girl asking you not to break down the door stopped you?"

"I didn't want to scare her."

Lindsey's frowning now. "Did she say anything at all?"

"Just that she wants to be left alone."

Her eyes soften as she places a hand on Kevin's shoulder. "Has your sister ever had her period before?"

Kevin's facial expression transforms from one of concern, to one of absolute horror in an instant. "How the heck would I know?" he cries. "Ew! That's so disgusting."

Lindsey smirks, as if he had just answered her question, and grabs her purse off of the counter. "I'll be back," she says as she makes her way up the stairs.

I hear the soft knock she makes on the bathroom door, along with their muffled voices.

Thinking about Lindsey's question, I shudder and pour myself another coffee. When I'd agreed to take these kids in, I didn't once think about periods. Hell, I hadn't considered a lot of things. Is that what this is? Did Natalie just get her first period? I'm so out of my element on this. Thank God for Lindsey.

"I can't believe we're missing school because of a stupid period," Kevin groans. Whatever worry he'd shown before is gone, only to be replaced with annoyance.

"We don't know for sure that's what it is," I say, plopping my ass down in a chair.

A slow smirk spreads across his lips. He's enjoying my misery. "You have no idea what you're doing, do you? Do you even know what to do for a period?"

"Do you?" Sighing, I drag my hand across my face. "I know enough. By the time Lindsey came along back when she was a teen, she was already getting hers. I just bought her what she told me to. It was never exactly a topic of conversation either of us wanted to discuss."

This makes him chuckle.

I reach out and place my hand on his shoulder. "Kev, I don't know much about being a parent. I think we all know that well enough. But I got a decent home, two extra bedrooms, and I would never let you or your sister down like your parents and your uncle did."

Kevin's smile disappears as tears form in his eyes.

"When you guys are experiencing your firsts, they're gonna be firsts for me too. But fuck it, ya know? Better to learn together than to learn that shit on our own, right?"

Kevin nods, his eyes shining with unshed tears. "Right."

Releasing his shoulder, I sit back in my seat. "And when it comes to girly shit like periods and new bras…" We both cringe. "Well, we'll let Lindsey handle that."

Kevin grins. "Agreed."

Just then, Lindsey steps out from the bathroom.

"Well?"

"We're going to need to make a run to the pharmacy, unless you have some extra maxi pads lying around."

"Why the fuck would I have those?" It's not like I've had a woman hiding out here. Not since Gina up and left, and that was two houses ago. Her shit was long gone after what she did.

Lindsey folds her arms over her chest and laughs. "Exactly. Why don't the two of you head to the store, and I'll help her get cleaned up. Get some ice cream too. Do you know what flavor she likes?"

"Mint chocolate, I think." Kevin shrugs. "Is she going to be okay?"

"She will be, Kev."

"Come on, son. Let's go get what we need for your sister, and we'll have a talk about why every man should be okay with picking up the feminine shit the women in our lives need."

Kevin scrunches his face at me. "Why would I do that? That's gross."

"Brownie points, kid. Brownie points."

## Grace

THIS CASE HAUNTED me all last night, to the point I didn't sleep a wink. When my alarm went off this morning, I was already dressed and out the door. The inkling that these two kids' story was worse than I feared nagged at me the entire drive to work. I tried to shake it off, but the feeling wouldn't dissipate.

I have to help them someway, somehow.

A few minutes past nine, my desk phone rings. I don't hesitate a single second to pick up when the school's name flashes across the caller ID on my desk phone. *Please, let them be there.*

"DFPS, Child Investigations Division. This is Grace."

"They're both here. The secretary at the school office tried to get the plate off the pickup truck that dropped them off, but they left too quickly." It would have been nice to have that information, but for now, the children being at school is enough for me.

"I'm on my way. Don't let them leave if you can help it."

"Why would they leave?"

"If there's something amiss with these kids, they could have eyes on them. We can't take any chances."

"Oh, goodness," she gasps. "Should I send our resource officer to their classrooms to gather them?"

"No, you might spook them. Just leave them be and keep an eye out. I'll be there as quick as I can."

Gathering a few things from my desk, including the case file I had put together with the two previous reports and photographs, I fire off a quick email to my supervisor, alerting him to the developments in the case. I don't wait for his reply before I'm out the door of my office and halfway down the stairs to the parking lot. With wide, determined steps, I find my sedan in its usual spot.

I hear Greg's voice calling out from the alleyway behind me. "Morning, Grace. Where's the fire?"

"I'm sorry, Greg, but I don't have time to talk."

"Figures. I came all this way to see you," he grumbles loud enough to hear.

"I'll make it up to you," I holler back, shoving myself into the car. "Milkshakes on Friday?"

"I'll hold you to it."

The last part comes out muffled after I close the door, but I can read his lips—strawberry. Firing up the engine, I take off in the direction of the school. The traffic is thankfully light for this time of morning, and I make it there in record time.

As I approach, the pale red brick building stands out against the more industrial nature of this area of town. Nestled near the back of the school's parking lot is an expansive football field that dwarfs the building entirely. If there's one thing about Texas, football is king here. This stadium is proof enough of that. If you could find a different state with more expansive football fields at the high school level, I'd be surprised.

A gray-haired woman stands outside of the main entrance of the school, nervously tapping her foot as I approach. Her eyes latch onto me almost immediately.

"Miss Halfpenny?" she inquires with a noticeable tremble in her voice. "I'm Ms. Pyle. We spoke on the phone earlier. I thought it would be best if I met you outside."

"You can call me Grace." I reach out to shake her hand, but she ignores it. Instead, she waves her petite one to the heavy metal doors and swipes the badge swinging from a lanyard on her chest against the reader. It beeps, and the lock clicks free. Opening the door, she beckons me inside.

"Follow me to my office. I just received the information you requested from their registration paperwork after we spoke."

She leads me to the back of the main office, just off the entrance, where the brick facade continues inside of the school. The worn tile floor desperately needs a good scrubbing. Once in the office, I spy several offices and one large receiving area, which is empty. Toward the back of the main area lies a much larger office. When we enter it, I find a younger woman seated in a chair across from the desk.

"This is Miss Crabtree. She was here when Kevin and Natalie were enrolled." Miss Crabtree smiles and extends her hand out to greet me with a limp shake. "Please, take a seat."

Settling into the open seat next to Miss Crabtree, I open up my case file on my lap and retrieve the images I had found from the other two cases and my tape recorder. Both of the women eye it suspiciously.

"Is that necessary?" Miss Crabtree questions.

"In child investigations, I'm required by law to record all conversations with the children. If you both consent, I'd like to also record your observations should I need additional evidence to get a court order if I deem it necessary."

"Of course," the superintendent agrees. "Miss Crabtree?"

"I suppose that's all right."

Setting the recorder down on the desk in front of me, I click the record button. "Case number 204678. Natalie and Kevin Tucker. Interview with school staff." I look up at the women. "I have two photographs I'd like to show you." Handing over the two images to Miss Crabtree, I allow her a few seconds to study them. "Do you recognize these children?" A part of me hopes these aren't the same kids, but the flash of recognition in her eyes douses that hope.

"She looks like the girl. A little younger, maybe, but she's got the same dark hair and sad eyes."

"And the boy?"

"I mean, he could be the same boy, but I'm not sure." She peers at it closely, but shakes her head. "Are these the Tucker kids?"

It's not implausible that Kevin had changed in the years since these photos were taken, but the resemblance of the girl means that, unfortunately, they're more than likely the same two kids who've already been in the system. A shame, really. The hope that their lives had improved for the better since their last stint in foster care is heartbreaking.

"I was hoping I was wrong, but I believe they are.

What can you tell me about the man who came with them on registration day?"

Pulling out a pad of paper and a pen from my briefcase, I place them both on top of the file on my lap.

"He was older," she remarks. "I guess late forties? Big beard." Her hands begin at her chin and move downward. "About to here, I think."

I jot down her observations. "Is there anything else you can tell me about him?"

"He was very rude when I called him about the enrollment paperwork and their previous records. Even more so when he came into the office about the matter."

"Could you go a little more into detail about that?"

"I believe he said, and I apologize for the language, 'Since when the fuck do you have to have shot records for kids?' He fought with me for several minutes before he said he'd bring me the paperwork later. He left after that."

"And did he provide that paperwork?" Records like this could be crucial in retracing the steps of both kids. We'd have more avenues of information gathering to pursue, at least. The principal clears her throat, and we both shift to look in her direction.

"When the IT department pulled the records on file for the kids with the registration paperwork you requested, these were in the system with it." She slides over a thin stack of papers to me.

"I thought you said he didn't bring you the paperwork?" I question Miss Crabtree, who shrinks back into her chair beside me. "If it's in the school's system, he would've had to bring it into the office. Am I correct?"

"He didn't. At least, I didn't see him again, but he might have brought them in while I was at lunch."

"I'd check with our normal administrative assistant, but she's been out sick this week. I'm assuming he left it with her." Ms. Pyle shrugs her shoulders. "Nevertheless, it's all in order."

I thumb through the top copy and find several pages of transfer records, and even a short medical record history for both children. The last page draws my interest the most, which has their guardian's name written in broad strokes: Eugene Grant. The address is a little harder to read, but the street couldn't be that far away from the school.

"I think this will do for now. I'll need to keep a copy of this paperwork for our records."

"It's all yours. We have the originals digitally held in our cloud storage."

"If that's all you need from me, I had the guidance counselor pull them from class under the guise of a new student orientation meeting. If you'll follow me, I'll introduce you."

"Will you please privately notify the counselor that I will be recording my interaction with the children?"

"I'll just send her a message now that we're on our way, and will let her know about the recording device." She types quickly on an open laptop to her left, smiling when she strikes the last key.

"She's aware, and they're ready for you."

With a polite nod to Miss Crabtree, I collect my files and tape recorder, and follow the superintendent to the closed office I'd passed earlier. Knocking quietly, she opens the door, apologizes for interrupting, and introduces me to the counselor, Mrs. Parks, who waves me inside. The second I walk over the threshold, two pairs of eyes focus intently on me, like they know I'm here for them.

Dear God. There's no doubt the images I have are of the same children sitting in front of me, their worry clear as day on their faces. The same eyes. Same faces. By all appearances, they look healthy, but physical health doesn't prove there's no physical abuse, if that's the case here.

Stepping inside the office, I nod when Ms. Pyle closes the door behind us. Taking the only available seat in the room next to Natalie, I tuck my briefcase beside my feet on the floor, but quickly conceal the recorder on the top of it, away from the kids' line of sight. She recoils back in her chair and leans closer to her brother, who's staring a hole right through me with angry eyes.

"Who's she?" Kevin mutters to the counselor.

"A friend," I reply sweetly. "My name is Grace. What's your name?"

"A friend would know our name," he fires back.

I smile. "Of course."

"Kevin Tucker," Mrs. Parks admonishes.

Kevin eyes me up and down, analyzing every inch of me, like he's one of those X-ray scanners at the airport looking for dangerous objects. He frowns, unamused at my assumption of being their friend. If I had been in the system for as long as they had, I'd be wary of anyone claiming to be my friend as well. I have to play this carefully, or risk losing the chance of speaking to them one-on-one. Well, one-on-two.

"I understand you're both new here. Did you just move?"

Natalie remains quiet, while Kevin rolls his eyes at me. "Why does that matter?"

"It's just a part of getting to know you both as new students," Mrs. Parks coolly lies. "Please answer the question, Kevin."

"Yes. We moved here a few weeks ago."

"With your family?"

Natalie shoots a puzzled look over to her brother before leaning in to whisper in his ear, but he shakes his head to silence her.

"With our uncle."

Uncle? What about their mother? She's their legal guardian, so for the kids to be living with another family member strikes me as odd. Curious, even, because not a single family member came forward to take custody of them when their mother had been arrested. If this uncle can take them in now, why didn't he previously? The more I think about it, the more the swirling pit of uneasiness unfurls inside of me.

It's plausible she handed over custody to their uncle, but we should've been notified with the change of status in their prior cases. A search of the court case records should give me insight into if it was legally done, but the problem will be if there is even a record at all. So many custodial parents with a history of drug abuse or criminal activity dump their kids on a family member's doorstep, never to be seen again. The key to all of this is finding out how they ended up with his man, and where their mother is.

"What's your uncle's name?"

"Jud—Uncle Eugene."

"Do you like where you live?"

His body tenses. *Too soon, Grace. Too soon. Get back on track.*

"You don't have to answer that if you don't want to, Kevin."

"Can we go back to class now? My sister and I have been sick. I don't want to fall further behind in our schoolwork."

The urgency to flee is obvious in his voice. He's uncomfortable with my line of questions. Mrs. Parks shoots over a concerned glare. I'm losing him, and pressing more might shut him down completely. I'm at a proverbial dead end until I can verify all the information now in my possession and speak with their uncle. My time is up.

"Seriously, can we leave now?" he asks, this time with a little more attitude as he gets to his feet and reaches out for his sister.

"It's okay, Kevin. You and Natalie can go back to class."

Without another word, they leave the room like it's been set on fire.

Mrs. Parks forces a smile. "I'm sorry. New schools can be overwhelming for older kids. I'm sure if you let him settle in, he'll be more forthcoming next time."

"Maybe," I lie, knowing that children from their backgrounds never feel safe around people like me. They see us as the devil knocking at their door, trying to steal them away from their family. Kevin knew exactly who I was. He could read me like an open book. You only get that kind of spatial awareness when you've been on the other side of the social services' coin.

With a polite "Thank you," I take my leave with the request that if they're absent within the next few days to call me. I'm lost in my own head when my body hits an immovable object when I step outside the main office.

"Miss Crabtree," I blurt out. "I'm so sorry. I didn't see you there."

"It's my fault. I've been waiting on you to leave the office so I could talk to you one-on-one."

"Is there something you didn't mention before?"

She blushes. "Yes. I was the one who made the call. I know I didn't leave my name, but I didn't want to risk my job, or my life."

"Your life? How could a call such as yours put your life at risk?"

Her gaze shifts away from me as she nervously chews on her bottom lip. "He's a biker. He had on this black leather vest with a logo on the back of it. You know, like the kind on television. It had the little patches on the front and everything. His said "Judge" on it."

"Did his vest have anything else on it? Like an insignia?"

Motorcycles were popular in our state with the year-round riding weather, but her notice of the name on the front of his jacket will be helpful to identify his club affiliation. Not that there were many clubs around here that I knew about, but I have to explore all the possibilities.

"It did," she whispers. "Black Hoods MC."

The feeling that had been festering in the pit of my stomach explodes at the mention of that particular club's name. The Black Hoods are notorious in Austin, and if they're somehow involved with these kids, my case just became much more complicated than just two kids without paperwork.

I thank her for her information, and the second I'm out the door, I retrieve my cell phone from my bag and type in a number for someone who might be able to help me now that bikers may be involved. I notice my recorder on the top of my bag, still recording. Her additional information became even more important now that I have it on tape.

"How's the prettiest girl in Texas?" his baritone voice almost coos into the receiver. "You ready to accept that offer of mine and go out on a date with me? My dancing boots have been itching for a night on the town with a pretty lady like you."

"Hey, Aaron." Aaron and I had met a few years ago when I'd been called to work one of his cases for the

Austin PD. He was a new hire at the time, and new to the area. After working together for a few weeks on the case, we'd struck up a rapport with each other.

"This isn't a social call, is it?" His tone tells me he's clearly disappointed.

"I wish it was, but I need your help. What do you know about the Black Hoods MC? I've got a new case they may be involved with."

His voice goes cold. "They're bad news, Gracie. If they're involved, you're going to need all the help you can get."

"That's precisely why I'm calling you."

## Judge

"THAT'S GREAT. THANKS, SHARON." Shoving my phone back into my pocket, I plaster a serious look on my face.

"What did she say?" Twat Knot asks, unable to take the silence any longer.

I sigh, as if I'm about to deliver bad news, but I can't hold back my own grin. "They accepted the offer. We got ourselves a new garage, boys. I'll sign later this afternoon and pay the lady."

Cheers and hoots of excitement fill the meeting room, and though I usually like to keep our church meetings serious and business related, I join in. This garage is exactly what this club needs.

Sure, we have a purpose. We help people in trouble when the police aren't doing their jobs, but that doesn't pay the bills. Buying this garage will offer endless possibilities for the members of this club and their families. A new venture to financially support the club, and to add a desperately needed amenity to the neighborhood, as well as a way to help our new members and kids get work experience.

"To new futures!" Karma declares, holding his beer bottle high over the center of the table.

"And more money!" Twat Knot cheers as everyone clinks their bottles together in celebration.

Once everyone has settled, I take my seat at the head of the table, motioning for the others to do the same. "We've been so busy taking care of everyone else, it's high time we take care of ourselves. We've worked hard for this, but now that we actually have the place, the hard work is just beginning."

"Figures," Twat Knot groans. I nod at Karma, who smirks and swats him across the back of the head.

"Things are about to get a lot busier around here, but the ride is going to be so fucking worth it. Who's with me?" More cheers echo through the room, and I grin, slamming the gavel down on the table, ending the formality of our meeting. "Another round of beers!" I call out.

Everyone piles out of the room toward where the beer is kept. I'm right behind them, but stop when my phone rings. The name on the screen sets me into an instant panic.

Accepting the call, I press the phone to my ear. "Kevin, is everything okay?"

"No, I don't think it is," he whispers.

I close the door to the meeting room, muffling the sound of excited bikers in the other room. "What's going on, kid?"

He continues to whisper. "There was some chick here today. She tried to tell us she was a friend. She was asking all kinds of questions about who we live with and who you are."

*Fuck.*

"Did she give you her name?"

"Grace. That's all she said. I didn't tell her anything, I swear. I don't think she works for the school, though. She looked like a social worker." He's seen enough of them to know.

Sighing, I rub my hand down my face. Figures. One good thing happens, only to immediately be followed by something bad. "It's all good, Kev. I'll look into it. You and your sister okay, though?"

"Yeah. Nat's back in class, and I'm headed to mine now."

"Good," I mutter, distracted now by thoughts of who this Grace bitch might be and why she's asking my kids questions at all. "Thanks for telling me, Kev. I'll deal with it, okay?"

"Yeah, okay. Bye."

As soon as the call disconnects, I go to the door and call out for Hashtag.

"What's up?" he asks, slipping into the room and closing the door behind him.

"Someone was sniffing around the kids at school, some bitch named Grace. Didn't give them any more info, but I got a bad feeling. Kevin said he was pretty sure she was a social worker."

"What do you need from me?"

Groaning, I lean my ass against the table. "I don't even fucking know," I admit. "Check the school personnel roster for a Grace, see if she even works there. Or see if there are any flags on their file. Something. Anything. I just got those kids, and I'll be damned if anyone's gonna take them away from me."

I'd lost my family once before, and I sure as fuck won't lose this one.

"Yeah, no problem. I'll see what I can find. Give me an hour."

Hashtag disappears as he heads toward his office.

Mom approaches me, looking concerned. "What's wrong?"

"There might be a complication with the kids."

"Need me to look into it?"

I clap my hand on his shoulder. "I appreciate it, man, but Hash is going to see what he can find out with that computer shit he does. Besides, you've got enough problems to deal with on your own. I can't ask you to take on anymore."

"You ain't fuckin' kidding. But if you need me, let me know. Crazy wife and all, I'm here for you and those kids."

"I appreciate it."

"I wish I could tell you it gets easier as they get older, but my kids are just like me."

"No wonder Marie's a fucking psycho. She lives with you and your clones."

His smile is genuine when he acknowledges, "Keeps life interesting."

A wail from the other side of the room draws our attention. Rushing out, we find Marie on top of one of the tables, dancing like a stripper on dollar dance night, gyrating her hips while the drink in her hand sloshes all over the table. Slipping, she lands flat on her ass, laughing, while Mom looks over to me and scowls.

"Woman's gonna send me to an early grave, I'm telling ya."

Shaking his head, he stalks toward her, yelling for her

to get her old ass off that table before she breaks her hip. The longer they're together, I swear, the crazier she gets.

She's still laughing when he hauls her off the table, but then her expression turns serious when he lays into her, and she slaps him hard across the face.

I don't envy him. I tried a relationship once, and it didn't work out. Ain't ready to try that bullshit again. I have enough on my plate with Kevin and Natalie, and there's no need to add anymore chaos to my nuthouse of a life.

## Grace

AFTER YET ANOTHER night of sleeplessness, I took a deep dive into web searching motorcycle clubs. From fictionalized shows on television to real-life clubs, my brain is pounding from information overload. The only thing I couldn't find much on was the Black Hoods MC specifically, apart from a few new articles about charity rides and mentions in local crime ring busts the last few years. Aaron's warning was clear about staying away from them, but this case may not allow for that to happen. I have to hope he can find out more information for me without putting myself in danger if I can help it. If I can't, so be it.

With the promise that Aaron would get back to me later today with the information I had emailed him after the call, I pull out the notes I'd scribbled down last night while listening back over the recordings.

The first thing on the list may be the most crucial piece of the puzzle. Where is their mother? And why did this so-called uncle have the kids? If things were on the up-and-up, there would be records. Looking up the number for the court clerk's office, I place the call. After a few rings, someone picks up.

"Clerk's office."

"Hi. My name is Grace Halfpenny, and I'm calling from DFPS. I need to have some court records pulled for a case I'm working on."

"Case number?"

"I have two previous case numbers in our system. Case Number 18746, and 19430."

I listen as the click of a keyboard fills the silent end of their receiver.

"I can have the records for these two cases couriered over to your office in a few hours."

"That would be great. I also need a search for any other cases involving the mother..." I trail off, looking at my notes. "Teresa Ann Tucker. DOB 7/31/1979. I'm specifically looking for cases regarding legal custody of her children."

"One moment, please." A few heavy-handed

keystrokes later, she informs me, "I don't have any additional records for a Teresa Ann Tucker with that DOB. Could she have had an alternate alias?"

My stomach drops. "Zero records?"

"Correct. The last two records for her in our system under that name were the two previous cases you mentioned."

Crap. She's a ghost in the wind, legally speaking. "What about the two minor children, Kevin and Natalie Tucker? Anything on them?"

After a few moments, she sighs. "Same for the children. Just the two previous records."

I stifle a curse. No record of the mother. No record of the uncle's custody. On top of everything else, this case just continues to snowball, going from bad to worse.

"Is there anything else you need?" she asks politely.

With a defeated tone, I reply, "No, that's it."

"The courier service will have these over to you soon. Have a good day."

She hangs up, and my head falls into my hand with the receiver still pressed against the side of my face.

"Everything okay?"

I peer up and see Aaron's thick stature leaning against the doorframe, cradling a stack of folders, his normally clean-shaven face showing a hint of dark stubble. His head looms nearly at the top of the door, but being almost seven feet tall would make any space look frighteningly small. Aaron's muscular build has grown larger since I last saw him. He's like a gentle giant with a cowboy hat and a pistol at his hip. It's no wonder he's done so well in law enforcement, as he certainly looks the part. If I was on the other side of the law against him, I'd have no chance of getting away.

His large boots step into my office and he turns, closing the door behind him before settling into one of my way too small desk chairs. His knees press against the front of my desk, like a parent trying to sit in their child's desk at a parent-teacher conference.

"Didn't know phones made good pillows." I narrow my eyes at him. "Bad morning?"

"I don't know how it could get any worse, to be honest. Please tell me you have some good news for me on the Tucker case?"

"I wish I did. I asked a couple of patrol officers to do a few more drive-bys of their compound, and the address you gave me last night to watch for the kids. So far, no dice."

"Shit."

"Wow." His eyes flash with surprise. "Grace Half-penny swearing? It *has* been a bad day."

It's not that I'm against swearing, but after years of living with a very strict Christian foster family in my early teens, their punishments for using said words still make me think twice about using them. Mama Marie, my foster mother, had a heavy hand for anyone who used them, or even a watered-down version of them.

"I'm sorry. It's this case. Between not sleeping and all these curveballs that keep getting thrown at my head, I'm unraveling a bit."

Leaning his gigantic frame forward, he takes hold of my hand, enveloping it wholly with his. "I know you want to help these kids, Gracie, but if your tip is right, anything to do with this club needs to be handled by the police."

"I can't do that, Aaron. I just can't. This is *my* case," I argue, taking my hand out of his. Sighing, he settles back into his seat. "I didn't call you for help because I can't handle it."

He recoils, like I just shot an arrow through his heart. I know Aaron has good intentions and wants to protect me, but I'm not backing down from this case, no matter who's involved. Bikers be damned. These kids deserve better, and if I can help them achieve that, I will.

"I'm sorry. I overstepped. You're right, this is your case, not mine. I didn't mean to pop by and make your day worse. That wasn't my intention."

"I know it wasn't, but I guess that brings us around to why you stopped by out of the blue." Outside of a few friendly lunches sparsely scheduled over the last few years, our friendship hadn't included random visits at our places of work.

"I pulled some records on the mother's past charges and thought I'd bring them over." He slides a manila folder over to me.

"And?" I tease him.

"And I wanted to invite you to lunch. It's been awhile, and I miss our visits." His tone is hopeful.

"I wish I could, Aaron, really, but my afternoon is jam-packed with calls and meetings, so I had planned on working through lunch."

His unmistakable disappointment breaks his normally cool and collected demeanor. "That's okay. I knew it was a long shot, anyway."

"What about tomorrow evening? I have court after lunch, and provided it doesn't run over, I can be out of here early."

A flash of excitement washes over his face as he smiles widely.

"It's a date. I'll make a reservation at your favorite place for six." I wish he hadn't used that word. It's a work meeting, nothing more. But the way he said it makes a coil of guilt swirl in the pit of my stomach. Dating is the last thing I have on my mind, and he'd be better off finding a woman who would appreciate him for the great guy that he is.

"If court goes long, I'll call you."

Pushing away from the desk, he smiles at me. "See you tomorrow, Gracie." Elation almost wafts off of him as he opens the door and heads out of my office.

Aaron has always been a good friend, but for me, that's all it is—friendship. Aaron's a great guy, but his line of work and mine don't make for a good relationship. We're both married to our jobs, and there's no room for anyone else in them, especially now with his recent promotion to detective. And I barely have time to sleep. Adding a second person in my life just isn't in the cards.

Shoving the thought from my mind, I return to my full case load for the rest of the afternoon. Meeting after meeting with current cases fill it to the brim before the last client walks out of my door around five thirty. My body is physically exhausted, and the idea of slipping into my clawfoot tub with a frosty glass of wine seems like the embodiment of heaven on earth. I check my email one last time before I gather up Aaron's folder, along with the one the courier had dropped off to me between meetings to peruse later tonight at home before leaving my office.

The sun's still beaming down with a Texas level heat, even this late in the day. Opening my car door, the interior heat flows out, feeling like a sauna. Normally, this late in the summer, things would start evening out temperature-wise, but Mother Nature seems hell-bent on making it stay miserably hot as long as she can. I should've known that little temperature break over the last few days would come back to bite me again.

I let the heat sift out before braving the scorcher still raging inside and crank the air the second the engine turns on. With my work ahead of me, and the thought of possibly sleeping later, I leave the parking lot when a large group of motorcycles swerve into the lane I was about to pull into without so much as even a wave of apology.

"What in the hell?" I mutter when one biker waves after he passes. I try to see a plate number to report them for cutting me off when my eyes spy the back of their vests.

They're not just any group of bikers. They're Black Hoods.

"Don't do it, Grace," I berate myself when the thought of following them pops into my head. "Aaron said they're dangerous. Following them isn't a smart move."

My heart beats wildly in my chest while my mind plays devil's advocate of toeing the dangerous line of inserting myself into their line of sight without a police escort. I could either be walking into my doom, or become the guiding light to helping these kids. Do I put my life on the line for them?

The light flicks to green. They take off, and so do I, right behind them.

This is either the bravest thing I've ever done or the stupidest. I'm leaning toward the latter.

## Judge

"YOU FUCKERS," I groan, but I can't hide my grin. "I'm a little old for a surprise party, don't you think?"

"You're too old for most things," Twat Knot quips. I nod to Karma, who lands a swift swat to the back of his head. "Don't worry, old man. Us young bucks will make sure the ladies don't give that old ticker of yours palpitations."

A gorgeous blonde with fake tits strides up to me and hands me a beer. "Happy birthday, handsome." Ladies love a silver fox, and at fifty, there's more silver in my beard than there ever has been.

"Thanks, sweetheart." She plants a kiss on my cheek, pressing her tits against my arm as she does it, then struts back into the crowd. I watch her go before turning to face the others.

"Now, who do I have to thank for this shindig?" Everyone looks away, avoiding eye contact at all costs. "Come on, ya bunch of bastards. Nobody knew shit about my birthday. Who was it?"

I narrow my eyes at Hashtag. Motherfucker.

He glowers back at me, and then finally throws his hands up in the air. "I had to enter your birthday when I did the paperwork for the kids. I thought it would be nice, okay? So drink your beer and enjoy the love, for fuck's sake."

I glare at him a moment longer. It's not that I'm upset, exactly. I just don't quite know what to do here. I've never had a surprise for anything. Hell, I've never had a birthday party. "Thanks, kid."

Nodding, he clinks his bottle against mine.

Taking a seat, I stroke my beard. "Fifty fucking years old, GP," I say. "That's half a fucking century."

Numbers had never bothered me before. But then, I'd never turned fifty years old before today, either. I motion for the waitress to bring another round before turning to watch the girls on the dance floor.

They're all so fucking young. I could be their damn grandfather. That shit is truly depressing.

"Cheer up, old man," Hashtag chuckles, clapping a hand on my shoulder. "Your present will be here soon."

I love my club, and they know I've been struggling.

First with Natalie and Kevin, becoming an instant dad to two damaged teenagers. And second, that I'm almost old enough to collect a fucking pension—if I had one.

That's why they'd suggested a new venue. They'd brought me to Sharkey's. This bar is perfect for a guy like me, or so they'd said. It had been once, about fifteen years ago, but now I feel like I should walk around, handing out condoms and ten-dollar bills to the barely legal boys staring at their first pair of fake tits.

"Excuse me?"

I turn to see who'd spoken, and take in the tall, slender woman in front of me. Her hair is pulled into a tight little knot at the back of her head, and her glasses are resting on the tip of her nose. She's wearing a business suit, the kind you see in movies with the sport coat and matching skirt. She looks like a librarian, but the girl is stacked, and that's when I realize just what kind of librarian she is.

"Halle-fucking-lujah!" I roar, looking around at my boys. "I thought you guys had gotten me something stupid, like a new helmet or a saddlebag for my ride, but this…." I look the librarian up and down with insurmountable approval. "Fucking hell. Happy birthday to me!"

The woman's eyes go wide as she takes a step back. "I beg your pardon?"

"Do you just do the show, or do you provide the after-party too?" I reach for her, wanting to feel her on my lap.

"Judge," GP blurts out from behind me.

"I don't provide any show, sir," she snaps back, her face twisted in anger. "And I don't like what you're insinuating."

Laughing, I take another swig of my beer. "I'm insinuating that I can't wait for you to take off that shirt and show me them gorgeous titties."

"Judge!" GP hollers, but it's too late.

The librarian's hand comes up and slaps the side of my face, hard enough to send my chair sideways.

"I will not be spoken to like that. My name is Grace Halfpenny, and I'm a caseworker for Child Protective Services. I'm looking for a man named Eugene Grant."

*Oh shit.* I sit up straight in my seat and place the beer gently down on the table. "I'm Eugene."

I ignore the snickers from the guys around the table as Ms. Halfpenny huffs and pulls a stack of papers out of her briefcase, plopping them onto the table in front of me. "Mr. Grant, it has come to my attention that you've been caring for a Kevin and Natalie Tucker without legal right to do so. Those children are wards of the state."

Realization washes over me that this is the Grace that was at the school. I may have offended her, but I don't like her tone when it comes to those kids. "Those kids are orphans who had nowhere to go. They've had a fucked-up few years, and the last thing they needed was to be separated and shoved into some goddamn foster home."

"Mr. Grant, you don't have the right to make that call."

I stand and move closer, using my size to intimidate her. "I will make whatever call I see fit. Those kids are happy with me, and that's how it's gonna stay."

Her nostrils flare, and I have to remind myself that she's a total bitch, because the look of her pissed off is one of the sexiest things I've ever seen.

"You haven't heard the last of me, Mr. Grant." Turning on her heel, she marches toward the door.

"I liked you better when you were a stripper!" I call out to her back, just trying to piss her off now.

It works. I smirk when my words stop her short, but she doesn't give me the satisfaction of seeing her sweat. Instead, she keeps walking, straight out the door, and hopefully out of my life for good.

*Yeah, right.*

"Wait," Twat Knot says with a laugh, clearly not getting the brevity of what has just happened. "Your name is Eugene?"

A nod at Karma shuts him up as he fends off yet another smack to the back of the head.

## Grace

"THERE SHE IS." Aaron smiles as the teenage hostess leads me to the table in the corner of the little Italian bistro we both love. His dark hair is slicked back, a stark contrast against his crisp white button-up shirt and dark trousers. The owner, Piero, steps aside as Aaron pushes up from his seat and pulls out my chair for me. I settle into it, placing my bag next to my feet on the floor.

*"Lei è bellissima."* Piero smiles, clapping his weathered hand onto Aaron's shoulder as a server approaches with a large bottle of wine and two glasses in his hand.

"Are we celebrating something?" I ask Aaron as the server pours us each a glass.

"A night with you is always a celebration, considering how many times you've cancelled on me lately," he teases.

"You know how much I work." An excuse, but a truthful one.

"So do I, but you can't forget to enjoy life. When you don't, all you see is the dark part of our line of work."

"I know, but—"

"But nothing. Piero picked out this wine especially for you. It's from his family's vineyard. Let's not spoil it with the same old argument we always have, darling." Picking up the glass, he swirls the dark merlot liquid in the glass before bringing it to his lips.

I scrunch up my nose. *Pet names?* When exactly did we make it to that level of familiarity in our friendship? The last time I checked, we were nowhere near that level. Catching my reaction over the brim of his glass, he frowns before taking another sip.

"Try it," he insists, trying to divert the awkwardness away from his slip.

I finger the stem of the glass before grasping it and bringing it to my lips. The plump, velvety merlot hits my tongue. It's good. One of the better wines I've had. But not even the alcohol sliding down my throat can deter me from his use of the word "darling".

"Like it?"

"I like it. I normally don't like merlots," I remark quietly. Merlots are his favorite, not mine. I'm more of a Moscato fan, but I don't want to insult him even more than I have by being almost an hour late. Court ran over, as I had expected it would. Mr. Jackson had somehow managed to get an earlier court date, but the judge ordered a continuance so he could review the matter further. His disapproval of the decision landed him with a charge of contempt of court.

"The usual?" Aaron asks, snapping me out of my caseload daydream.

"Sure."

"We'd both like the cacio e pepe."

"Of course, sir." The server scribbles away on his notepad before taking the menus from the table.

"I'm going to take a wild guess here, but court didn't go well, did it?"

"It didn't. But I thought you didn't want to talk shop during our meal?"

"Touché. It's like you don't think I know you that well. You're only meeting me tonight to find out more about the Tucker case."

"That's not true," I fire back, panicking at being caught red-handed. "I like Piero's just as much as you do."

Aaron slumps slightly into his chair. "I just wish it was the company you were as excited to see as it was the case file I have for you."

"You found something?" I almost gasp, making the

tension between us grow colder. I didn't even notice the folder sitting next to his plate with his hand resting on it until he mentioned it.

"I did." He passes the folder across the table, and I have to force myself not to snatch it out of his hand. I don't want to be greedy, but what he found could blow my case wide open. "But I have to warn you, there're some graphic photos in there. It might be best to save looking through it until after dinner."

"Oh. The mother?"

"Yes. I found her death certificate. She was originally logged as a Jane Doe until she was identified a few weeks later by her fingerprints in the IAFIS system. They found her at a truck stop."

Those poor kids. If their mother is dead, how in the world did they end up with this uncle? Next of kin determination, or did he just claim them?

"It gets worse, Gracie. A local lot lizard found her in a ditch near the back end of Ricky's truck stop off of I-35 and called it in. She had enough heroin in her system to kill an elephant. She OD'd."

A tidal wave of sadness washes over me. "That poor woman," is all I can get out. Addiction never leaves you. It takes an ugly hold around every aspect of your life and wrings you dry, until there's nothing left. "Did you find anything about what happened to the kids?"

"I spoke with the lead investigator this morning, who ran her death investigation. He didn't even know she was a mother, so that rules out that DFPS or law enforcement had anything to do with the current placement of either child."

"Shit. Shit, shit, shit."

Aaron's brows lift in surprise. "That's a lot of swearing for you in one sentence."

"It's got to be those bikers. There's no other explanation. She got caught up with them and OD'd. When she died, they took her kids with them. Nothing else makes sense. I knew I should've pressed that man further." I mutter away to myself, trying to work it all out while totally forgetting I hadn't planned on telling Aaron about my little adventure into the strip club a few days ago.

Aaron's body grows still. "You talked to them?"

"I might have," I answer sheepishly.

I listen for the ringing bell that should be dinging, because this dinner is about to go DEFCON now. Aaron has always been protective of me, but I haven't exactly thrown myself into the lion's den of danger with a group of men like the Black Hoods before. It's a first for us both, and the way he's staring a hole through me right now tells me all I need to know about how he feels over my little folly.

"After everything I told you about them, you still

went there? They could have killed you, Grace. Those men, that group. They don't care who they kill, as long as it serves their purpose."

"I don't even know why I followed them into that strip club, but I did." Lord have mercy, *mouth*. Connect with my brain already. If I could facepalm myself right now for my lack of a verbal filter, I would. Why did I tell him that too?

"A strip club? Jesus, Grace! What were you thinking?"

"I wasn't, but I had to find that man."

"I don't like this," he declares. "You're obsessed with this case. I knew you were one hundred percent dedicated to your job, but this,"—he waves his hands in front of him—"this nonsense will get you killed. You need to leave it alone and let me handle it. Let anyone else handle it."

Feeling scolded, I look down at the table, avoiding his gaze. "Those kids have no mother, no father. They only have me to look out for them."

"Risking your life isn't worth it. Not to the people who love you."

*Love.* That word between us gives me an uneasy feeling. He can't love me. He knows I don't love him, right? It has to be the heat of the moment talking. He doesn't know what he's saying.

"Grace, you can't be involved in this case. It's going to get you killed. Don't you see that?"

I finally meet his eyes. "That's for me to decide, isn't it? The last time I checked, I've never had a father in my life, and I'm not in the market for one now. I can make my own decisions just fine."

He stills at my tone, but his fermenting rage lingers on his face.

"You have a death wish if you think going headlong into that club is going to give you the answers you need. Those men are killers."

"And yet, here I am in one piece." He's treating me like a child. Was it stupid to walk into that strip club without so much as a gun to protect me? Of course it was. But that gray-haired brute of a man needed to know that his club didn't intimidate me. Nothing will stop me from protecting those kids. Not Aaron, and certainly not Eugene Grant and his band of bikers. I'm my own mistress, and there will be no fucking master, friend, or whatever he is, if he can't support my decision.

Anger wafts off him in thick waves, and as his voice raises, more eyes peer over at us. He's making a scene for the entire restaurant.

"Grace," he growls. "Please, leave it alone."

"No. End of story."

Coming over with our meals, the server quietly places

them in front of us as we both stew in our anger and frustration. I try to eat, but the longer I sit here, the angrier I get. When the server comes back by to check on us, I ask for a box. Aaron snaps out of his quiet rage, and something flashes in his eyes, something I've never seen before. He's hurt. I've hurt him.

"You don't have to leave on my account." His tone says the opposite. He's angry with me, but he's trying too hard to mask it. I know he cares about me, but he has to realize there's nothing between us. "Please, stay and eat your dinner."

"I can't, Aaron. After all of this, you know I can't."

Reaching for my purse, I grab a twenty and place it on the table to cover my half of the meal and wine. The server brings a box to the table and deposits my untouched meal into the Styrofoam container before handing it to me in the bag. I carefully place the file into my bag, grab my leftovers, and shove up from my chair. I move to walk away, but he reaches out and grabs my arm.

"Don't do this, Grace. Please." I jerk from his grasp and leave him alone to eat his meal. I don't look back.

Fat tears run down my cheeks as soon as I get outside, my chest heaving as a pang of anger roars out of me the second I'm away from him. Tonight is a major turning point in our friendship. Likely the end of it, I think. Aaron doesn't easily forgive, and leaving him there like that, I might as well have plunged a knife into his heart. Mine too, if I'm being honest. For so many years, I've relied on him like a crutch when things got tough. Maybe a little too much. It may hurt right now, but this is for the best, for both our sakes.

## Judge

"UH, GENE?" I turn to find Kevin standing in the doorway to the garage, his basketball resting against his hip. He nods his head toward the street, and I follow his gaze to see Grace Halfpenny climbing out of her car, her bun wound so tight at the back of her head, I'm surprised her skin isn't peeling off.

"Inside, bud."

"But—"

"Inside," I repeat. Shoving past him, I move to intercept her before she comes too far onto my property. Her eyes lock with mine, but her steps never falter as she moves closer. I hate that her skirt fits her figure so well.

"Mr. Grant," she says, extending her hand for me to shake.

Glancing down at it, I curl my lip in mock disgust. "What the fuck are you doing here?"

Her hand drops. "I thought I'd maybe try a do-over of our conversation from the other day."

I glower at her, totally ignoring the perfectly placed freckle just above her lip. "Do they actually pay you to fuck with people's lives?" Pulling my wallet from my pocket, I find a crisp hundred-dollar bill and offer it to her. "Here, take this for your time. Now leave."

She bristles at that. "Mr. Grant, my job is to ensure that all children are free from abuse and taken care of. That is my only goal, ever."

"Well, good then. End of discussion and job well done. Kevin and Nat are being well taken care of, and I personally see to it every single day that they're both free from abuse. You can go on your merry little way and find someone else to fuck with."

She sighs. "That's not the way this works."

"That's exactly the way this works. I'm not gonna bend over and let some bitch from DFPS come between me and my kids."

"They're not your kids, Mr. Grant."

Finished with her and her bullshit, I jam a finger in front of her face and lean in close. "They're more mine than yours. You don't know them at all, and I'm supposed to let you come in and take them off to some foster home run by strangers? Fuck that shit."

"They need to have a *legal* guardian, and all I need is for you to prove that's what you are, legally."

My blood boils. "You and I both know that ain't gonna happen. But neither is you taking those kids outta this goddamn house."

"I don't—"

"You think some overwhelmed foster parent is going to know that Natalie can't sleep without the light on? Or that Kevin needs a fan running in his room all night long?" She stares at me, her mouth hanging open. "Will they know that Natalie hates apple juice, but will devour an entire bag of apples as long as you slice them up for her?"

She swallows. "No, but—"

"Will they know that Kevin wants to play football but has never had anyone care enough about him to teach him how? And if they did, would they spend hours in the backyard teaching him, just like I do every single fucking night?"

I'm shaking with frustration and anger as she opens her mouth to speak and then closes it. Pressing her lips together, she tries again. "Look, Mr. Grant, I'm not here to argue the validity of the foster care program with you. I'm here to make sure these kids are in your home legally.

And until we can make it legal, we need to come up with a solution."

I glare at her. "Oh yeah? And what exactly is your solution?"

She squares her shoulders and looks me in the eye. "I need you to hand over the children to me and allow us to investigate the matter further. If you are in fact their next of kin, the children will be returned to you immediately."

"And if not?"

I'll give her credit; she doesn't miss a beat. "They will be placed in a home that can care for them until such a time that a relative comes forward or prospective adoptive parents can be legally vetted and approved."

Is she listening to her own fucked-up words? "So you're telling me you want to remove two orphan kids from a home they're happy in, loved in, and are part of a family that doesn't inject poison into their veins every fifteen minutes, taking them to some house where the parents are paid to keep them fed and clothed, but couldn't care less about who they are and how they feel?"

She blinks back at me, and miracle of all miracles, actually seems to be at a loss for words.

"Nah. You'll take these kids out of my house over my dead body."

The way she shakes her head seems to reek of defeat,

but I can tell by looking at her that she doesn't give up easily.

Reaching into a folder, she pulls out a card. "Take this," she says, her jaw set just as tight as mine. "It's my number and email address. You know I can't let this go, Mr. Grant. This isn't over. But if you change your mind and want to cooperate, please call me, and we can hopefully work together. I want this process to be as painless as I can for both Kevin and Natalie."

I snatch the card out of her hand. "If you take them away from me, it'll be far from painless."

"Have a good afternoon, Mr. Grant."

She holds herself together as she makes her way to her sedan, but I can see a slight tremble to her slim frame. I've rattled her.

She doesn't look back as she climbs into the vehicle, and she doesn't linger. Starting the car, she pulls away from the curb, and I watch until she's gone from sight.

"She's going to put us in a foster home, isn't she?"

I spin around and find Kevin and Natalie standing in the doorway to the garage, their eyes filled with worry. A tear escapes Nat's eye, gliding lazily down her cheek.

"*She* isn't putting you anywhere. This is your home." They don't look convinced, and quite frankly, I don't blame them, because I'm not convinced either. "Come on," I say, walking between them and draping an arm over their shoulders. "Let's get inside and see what we can find for supper, okay?"

They both move with me, allowing me to assuage their fears for now, but it's not until Natalie's head rests against my chest as we walk that I make my decision. If Grace Halfpenny shows up here again, she and the case file she lords over us may just have to disappear.

## Grace

BETWEEN EUGENE GRANT and Mr. Jackson's incessant calls regarding the continuance of his case, I'm nearly at my wits' end. Well, the end of the wits I still have left at my disposal. At this point, I'm sure my wits have flown the coop in search of a better brain to inhabit. Where Mr. Jackson is fighting for his rights, Mr. Grant seems to get off on frustrating me, enjoying the volley between us a bit too much.

At first, I thought his demeanor at the strip club was only because I took him by surprise, but really, it's all him. It's not a show of intimidation. His bulging muscles and height did that all on their own. It's the way he carries himself that grinds at me. His confidence. His determination that those kids belong to him without a single shred of evidence to prove otherwise. The way he takes up all the air around him, leaving absolutely nothing for anyone else to breathe. The fact that I like it in an odd way, something I've never felt before in all the cases and men like him I've had to go toe-to-toe with over the years. Nothing makes sense when it comes to Eugene Grant.

A part of me notices just how much he seems to love those kids, even when he's trying to press every aggravating button I have all at once.

On top of it all, Aaron hasn't called. Not that I'm surprised with the way I left things at the restaurant. In such a lonely world, he's been my only true friend, apart from Greg. He was my rock and sounding board when a case threw me for a loop. He didn't deserve to be left there like that, and the guilt has been eating me up inside ever since. I've picked up my phone a dozen times over the last few days to call or text him like I normally would, but I could never let myself dial the number. We've fought before, but never like this. I have to give him space.

A part of me misses him hovering around, but it's a bit of a relief to not have to explain my every move to him about this case. More so now that I went in person, unofficially, to speak with Eugene Grant again. He'd have locked me up if he knew and then he would throw away the key in his effort to protect me.

I've taken the time to dive deeper into the files Aaron had given me at dinner, though. Natalie and Kevin's mother didn't leave this world kindly, going by the photographs Aaron had included. Her sunken eyes and rail thin body lying in the ditch near the truck stop shook me more than I care to admit. I've seen things, horrible things, but her death... It'll haunt me for the rest of my life because when I look into her sad death stare, all I can see is Natalie and Kevin looking back at me.

Their pain.

Their terrible childhood.

How similar their upbringing is to my own.

Flipping through Aaron's files again, I find where I left off the night before and dive into my work. My notebook is filled with page after page of scribbles—notes, personal thoughts, and possible reasons for why they ended up with the president of a motorcycle club. All of them circle back to Eugene Grant. He's the key to everything.

My mind drifts off for a few seconds, considering all the secrets he must hold before my desk phone snaps me out of it. I blink twice when I recognize the number that comes across the screen. Aaron.

"H—Hi. I didn't expect you'd call me—"

"I have some information for you about the Tucker case." No hello. No sweetness in his voice. It's cold as ice. "There's been a missing persons report filed for the kids and an uncle. I emailed it all over to you."

"Let me open up my email." Clicking the icon, I find it at the top. "Got it. Do you have any information about the person who filed it?"

"Their father." He gives me no further information.

"Father?" I flip through the paperwork in front of me. "In all the case files, there's no indication of their father being in the picture. He's never sought legal custody."

"That's what I was told by the officer who took the report. All the information is there, as well as how to contact him. I put in an order for a background check since I knew you'd ask. They'll send the results directly to you."

"Thank you for sending this over to me, Aaron. Listen, I'm really sorry about what happened at the restaurant."

"Sorry, Grace, but I have to go." He hangs up without so much as an acknowledgment of my apology. I knew I had hurt him, but this seems so final. Am I truly losing my best friend over a case?

I allow myself a few minutes to compose myself before clicking on his email. The summation of the report from the officer who took it is sparse. Details are clearly not his forte. Kevin and Natalie's name, along with a Randall McDade, are listed as the missing persons by one

Mr. Henry Wayne Tucker. His contact information lies at the bottom of the report, now under review by the detective staff. Grabbing my phone, I dial the number.

"What?" a gruff voice barks into the receiver. "If you're selling something, I ain't interested."

"Are you Henry Wayne Tucker?"

"Who's asking?"

"My name is Grace Halfpenny, and I'm with the Texas Department of Child Protective Services. I was alerted to your recent missing persons report and wanted to inquire about it. Do you have a few minutes to talk to me?"

His tone immediately changes, all business now. "Yes, ma'am. My kids and my ex-brother-in-law, Randall."

"When was the last time you saw them, Mr. Tucker?"

"It's been years since I saw the kids. Their mother left one night with them, and I haven't seen them since. It's only recently that I found out they've been living with her brother. I went by his house, but it's gone. Burned to the ground. That's why I filed the report."

"I see," I murmur, trying to calm my racing heart.

"I lost everything when she left. My wife. My kids. My business."

The case records I have would dispute his claims, but his wife had been a drug addict, and unfortunately, with addiction, there's always a sob story. It's completely possible that she lied to us. It's not like it hasn't happened before, but it begs the question: why reach out now, after all these years? When the kids were placed into foster care, it was clearly marked that attempts to find another legal guardian were made and failed. There was no reason at the time to doubt their father wasn't in the picture. Until now.

"Your business?" I inquire.

"Family business with Randall. With my wife gone, he cut me out completely." The way he says "family business" strikes an odd chord with me. How could his wife leaving him affect a business partnership he had with her brother? Legally, he'd have every right to the business if he'd been listed on the legal documents.

"What was the nature of your business, Mr. Tucker, if I may ask?"

"It was... a moving company," he replies, stumbling over his words. "But that's not why I filed the report. I want to know what happened to my kids." The change in direction of the conversation, diverting away from the business is odd. Very odd.

"Can you tell me the ages of your children?"

"What does that matter? They're my kids." His agitation is obvious, but a father should know the ages of his children, even if they aren't in his life. The feeling hits me again, an uneasiness stirring deep in my gut. I know exactly where his children are, but something's warning me not to tell him.

"I understand that, sir. However, I must caution you that if the children are located, they will have to go into foster care until a DNA test confirms that you are, in fact, their father."

"They're my kids, my flesh and blood. I want them back. They belong to *me*. I have fucking rights to them."

"Then a paternity test will prove you're their father, and you'll be able to petition the court for custody."

He mumbles something inaudible, and then tells me, "Just find my kids, lady."

"I will let you know if we're able to locate them," I lie.

## Judge

"HAPPY BIRTHDAY, dear Natalie. Happy birthday to you."

The round of singing is enough to make me cringe, but the look on Nat's face is totally worth it. I watch her cheeks blush a deep pink as she leans over the picnic table in front of her and blows out the thirteen candles on her cake.

Applause and cheers erupt all around us, and I turn to look at everyone. The yard at the side of the clubhouse is packed. Every single member is here tonight. If they got kids, they brought them. There are friends of the club, and friends of friends of the club, and all of them are here to celebrate this gorgeous kid's birthday. I can tell by the look on her face that she's never had this kind of a fuss made over her in her life.

"Present time!" Lindsey squeals, pushing her way to the table with a stack of brightly wrapped boxes in her arms. She moves to set them on the table, and that's when all hell breaks loose.

Sirens wail from behind us, and I turn to see a SWAT van, followed by five police cruisers, and a car I recognize as Grace Halfpenny's, roar into the parking lot, their lights flashing.

Men and women in full-on SWAT gear pile out of the vehicles as if they're heading into battle, guns drawn and at the ready.

"Get on the ground!" they shout, their words echoing off the surrounding buildings.

It's utter chaos. Women scream. Natalie's eyes lock with mine. There's so much fear in them, it kills any chance I might have had in keeping my cool in this situation.

"What's going on here?" I bellow as two armed men approach me with their guns pointed at my head.

"Get on the ground," the closest man orders, getting nearer by the second.

I glance back at Natalie, Kevin, and Lindsey, who stand with their backs pressed against the picnic table, the younger two clutched in Lindsey's arms.

Fuck.

Slowly, I drop to my knees next to Karma. The others

are on the ground all around me, having dropped where they stood.

"Ain't a party till the cops show up," Karma says, likely trying to lighten the mood. But considering this was a party for a thirteen-year-old girl, the joke falls flat.

When I glance behind me, I see Lindsey on the ground, but the kids are nowhere to be found. My niece, God bless her, meets my eyes and nods with reassurance. She sent the kids to slip away, unseen.

One man wanders from one side of the crowd to the other, his pistol in hand. Besides his Kevlar vest, he's dressed in jeans, a dress shirt, and cowboy boots. "What the fuck is this all about?" I growl when he gets closer.

"There's the man of the hour," he says, squatting low so he can get a better look at me. "Bet you're wishing you'd given those kids over to DFPS now, aren't you?"

I narrow my eyes, but before I have time to say a word in response, Grace Halfpenny's plain black, high-heeled shoes appear in front of me.

"That's enough, Aaron," she snaps. "This is way more than I asked for. Why do you have them on the ground? We're here to get a couple of kids, not bust a bunch of bikers for drugs."

The cop, whose name appears to be Aaron, sighs. "Grace, I've told you already. These men are dangerous."

He's about to find out just how fucking dangerous I am.

"Enough!" she snaps again, this time dismissing him completely. "Mr. Grant, I'm here to relocate the children to a foster home in town until we can complete a formal inquisition into the best place for them. I never intended for it to be quite this big of a deal, and for that, I apologize."

"You're not taking those kids anywhere," I say, slowly getting to my feet. One officer moves to stop me, but Grace lifts a hand, indicating for him to leave me alone.

"I'm sorry, Mr. Grant, but I have a warrant. Those children are coming with me."

Every spark of attraction I've ever felt for this woman disappears in an instant. Everything disappears. "You fucking bitch. You miserable fucking bitch."

For a split second, she looks as if I've slapped her directly across the face, but she recovers quickly and turns to walk away, heading for the door of the clubhouse, and straight for my kids.

"No!" I explode.

Everything becomes a blur. A blur of anger, of rage. A blur of fists and blood, and the sound of flesh pounding flesh. Twice I have to redirect one of my own, as Ms. Halfpenny nearly gets caught in the crossfire.

Did she cause this fight? Yes. Am I going to let anyone hurt her? Not a fucking chance.

Stone Face and Twat Knot are guarding the door, more than happy to get their blows in while they do it, but when an officer pushes Karma, he slams against Grace, and I catch her just before she hits the wall.

"Are you okay?" I ask, turning her to face me. And then I feel the cold steel pressed against the back of my head and freeze. Raising my hands, my eyes zero in on Grace, who looks terrified for me.

## Chapter 15

Grace

"IT'S HER FUCKING BIRTHDAY, ASSHOLE," he yells as Aaron shoves him into the squad car while he pleads with me. He squirms in the backseat, still fighting against the cuffs wrapped around his large wrists. The way he looks back at me through the windows of the squad car may haunt me for the rest of my life, his sadness and rage all too clear.

"Coming here was a mistake," I tell Aaron. "We should've done this quietly and at his home. Not here."

"They sent us to execute the removal order. Why does the location matter? We neutralized the biggest threat. Now we can get the kids and be done with this." His tone implies his true intent. *I'll* be done with this. That's all he cares about. Not the kids. Not the additional trauma we've just unnecessarily inflicted on the both of them. I narrow my eyes at him.

"Don't look at me like that. I told you these guys were dangerous. You should be glad I came along." Yeah, *glad*. That's the word I'd use to describe his involvement. Powder keg would be more like it. I knew Mr. Grant would fight us, I just didn't think he'd fight this hard. He cares about these kids, and that makes him even more dangerous to the father's case. *If* he's their father. "This is just another case, Grace."

"Why are you even here? You're a detective." A patrol officer is normally the only one who accompanies me. The fact the warrant fell into his lap when it came across from the judge means he's meddling more in my cases than he's letting on. Every ounce of guilt that I felt for leaving him at that restaurant evaporates. He's letting his attraction for me dip into his professional career. And mine.

"To that little girl, it matters." A tear slips down my cheek, and Aaron zeroes in on it. He's never experienced trauma like this, but I have. His childhood was sunshine and rainbows compared to hers. To mine. If he had seen the terror on her face like I had, he might be more compassionate. Natalie will never forget this, and neither will I. "I try to make removals as painless as I can, and you turned it into a bull in a china shop. Or, in this case, a biker's clubhouse."

The smirk on his lips as we watch the squad car drive off together irks me. He's proud of himself for sending Mr. Grant off to jail. He's practically beaming. I turn to head toward the crowd when his hand reaches out, grasping my elbow.

"She'll be fine. The sooner she and her brother are away from these people, the better off she'll be. The boy too."

"If that helps you sleep at night, sure, but we both know the escalation of violence is on your head, not mine."

"Grace, that's not what I did."

Turning back, I get in his face. "That's exactly what you did. Instead of letting me do my fucking job, you took over. You did this," I hiss. He recoils at my rage, something he's never seen before. If dinner the other night didn't put a knife in our friendship, this did. If he wants to interfere with my job, puppet mastering his way into my cases, it's over. Done.

"Why are you still here? You did what you came to do."

"To protect you," he argues, his frustration getting the better of him. "His people are still here."

"And yet not one of them has incited violence against

me, have they? Your job is done. Let me do mine without any more of your special kind of help."

Storming off, I head toward the officer posted at the door of the building, peering over my shoulder once to see Aaron sliding into his car.

"My team swept the place. The kids aren't inside," the officer advises me when I approach. "One of the ladies ushered them inside while the fight broke out."

"What do you mean, they aren't inside?" A weight settles in my chest.

"I swept the house myself, went room to room. There's no one in there."

"Where's the woman you saw take them inside? Find her, now!"

He does as he's told. Every second that he's gone, my panic spreads. A short while later, a woman with a mop of brightly colored hair appears with him.

"Where are they? Where are the kids?"

She arches her brow at the question, but I don't miss the flash of panic in her own eyes that mirrors my own as she glances behind me.

"I'm not going to ask you again. Where are the kids?"

"They're in my uncle's room down the hall," she sneers, pointing to a hallway near the bar. She starts for the direction she's indicated, and I'm hot on her heels. She disappears inside before I can catch up, and I hear her yelling for both of them by name, switching between the two conjoined rooms.

"Natalie! Kevin! You need to come out now!"

No one answers back. Once I'm inside, she's on her hands and knees, peering under the large king-size bed that takes up most of the room. Pushing up off the floor, her body goes stiff when we both notice the open window.

"The window," she cries, rushing toward it. Leaning out of the opening, she jerks back inside a few seconds later.

"This is all your fault!" she screams at me. "They were happy until you came here, and now they're gone. You did this. You did this!"

"Issue an APB for them. They couldn't have gotten far," I order the officer before rushing out of the room.

My stomach drops to the floor. I've lost them. I let my argument with Aaron get in the way of my job and I lost them. She's right. This is all my fault.

Chapter 16

## Judge

"FUCKING DICK," I snarl as Grace's little cop lover slams the bars closed between us.

"Cool it, Grant, or the charges will just keep piling up."

"Fuck you."

He smirks and walks away, his cowboy boots echoing off the ceramic tile floor.

Son of a bitch.

I move toward the bed, and that's when I notice a man lying on the top bunk. We make eye contact for a brief second, but neither one of us says a word. Laying down on the bottom cot, I stare at the bunk above me.

Why the fuck had they come in with guns drawn like that? That's not typical police procedure. And why did that asshole seem to be so close to Grace? Why the fuck do I even care?

"What I wouldn't give for a beer, right?" the guy above me states.

The last thing I want to do is get into a round of small talk with some asshole in lockup, so I don't respond.

"These fuckers would get a lot more cooperation from me if they offered that on their menu."

Draping my arm across my eyes, I try to calm myself down.

"Oh, I get it. We're playing the 'I'm a tough guy, and I'm going to ignore this asshole' game. Okay. Got it."

"Jesus, man. Can you not take a fucking hint?"

Chuckling, he swings his legs over the side of the bed and jumps down.

"Look, I've been in here three times in the last two weeks. I'm bored out of my fucking mind, and I would rather think about anything else besides what I have going on in my life right now. So yeah, I can take a hint. But I don't fucking want to."

There's nothing menacing in the way he's holding himself, but lying down while he looms over me makes me uncomfortable. Yet one thing he said has kind of got me wondering.

Sitting up on the edge of the bed, I scowl over at him. He's tall. Almost as tall as Karma, who measures well over six and a half feet. His eyes are dark and bloodshot, and his hair is a straggly mess.

"What the fuck could you have done to get your ass in this cell three times in two weeks?" This is just a holding cell. It's not like this is county lockup. Whatever he's done isn't big enough to warrant a stint in there, but has surely pissed someone off enough to have him rotting away in here for a few days.

"Contempt of court, and harassing a couple of public officials will do that to ya." He reaches out his hand, the word SOUL tattooed across his knuckles. "Ty. Ty Jackson."

I grip his hand in mine. "Judge."

Ty nods and glances at the patch on my cut as I stand. "Prez of the MC, huh? Pretty sweet gig."

I snort as I wander over to the door. I can see the officers talking on the other side of a glass wall, but there's no sign of Officer Dickhead, or of my lawyer.

"Yeah. If you call babysitting a bunch of toddlers with tattoos and biceps a sweet gig, then I guess it is."

We spend the next twenty minutes shooting the shit. I'm not one to share my entire life's story, and I'm thankful he isn't, either. We talk about motorcycles and women, and our favorite BBQ joints to grab a decent steak.

And that's when Officer Fuckface opens the door to

our cozy little getaway. "Come on, Grant. We have some questions for you."

I glower at him as he cuffs me. *Fucking pussy.*

He leads me down a long hall and through a couple of different bullet-proof doors before finally turning into a room with one-way glass and a table in the middle. Grace is already seated at the table with her briefcase at her side.

She stands as I enter, and I can't help but notice the stray strands of hair that have escaped that tightly wound bun on top of her head. It looks wild and unkempt. It looks sexy as hell.

Fuckface shoves me down into a hard metal chair across from her and leans his ass against the table.

"What do you know about Randall McDade?" This fucker is clueless. Aren't they trained at some school for tight-asses to form a false friendship with their suspects? Since when do they cut right to the chase?

I feign ignorance. "Who?"

He leans in closer. "Randall McDade. He was the legal guardian of those kids. But lo-and-behold, he's missing."

"Aaron," Grace chides from behind him, but he ignores her.

"How did you get involved in this, Grant? How did you come into possession of two teenage kids with a dead addict for a mother, and an uncle who's suddenly MIA?"

I glare at him, but I don't answer.

"Aaron, let me talk to him."

Fuckface's jaw hardens, but he doesn't look her way. Instead, he attempts to stare holes into my head with his eyeballs. But, since that's not possible, he basically just sits there, looking like an asshole.

"Where's my lawyer?"

"On his way," Grace answers, having to lean around Aaron for me to see her face. "Your buddy... what's his name? Mom? He said to let you know he called the lawyer, and he's on his way."

I watch her, surprised she told me that at all, considering the situation at the moment.

"I want to talk to Miss Halfpenny, alone," I tell Officer Douchebag.

"Over my dead body, Grant. This is an investigation."

"Into what?" I growl. "I don't even know what the fuck you're talking about. You showed up on club property, threatening to shoot us all, and not once did you explain yourself. So, tell me, Nipple Dick, what the fuck are you investigating?"

His nostrils flare. "We have a report of a missing person, and we believe you know something about that."

"Are you charging me with something?"

He's got nothing, and he fucking knows it.

"I want to talk to Miss Halfpenny," I repeat.

Officer Cockstroker leans in real close, his nose nearly touching mine. "Not happening."

I roll my eyes. I could snap this asshole like a twig if I weren't in handcuffs. "Nice little pet ya got here, Half-penny. Do you get him to arrest all loving parents that care for the kids you're looking into?"

Grace blinks, her pouty lips parting in surprise.

"I don't," she says after a moment, and then pushes a paper toward me to read. "I've been in contact with a man who claims to be Natalie and Kevin's biological father. A paternity test needs to be done to confirm, but if he is who he says he is, those children cannot stay with you, Mr. Grant."

She may as well have sucker punched me right in the heart. "Father? But they don't have a father."

She shrugs, looking almost apologetic. "I'm looking into it, but you aren't making it easy for me to do my job."

"Fuck your job," I snap. "Your job is to take those kids out of a happy home and stuff 'em in with some stranger they don't even know."

"Not a stranger," she clarifies. "Their father."

"He's a fucking stranger to them. They don't even know his damn name."

Grace purses her lips, and for the first time, I think I see her waver. She does everything so by the book, always carrying herself with an air of professionalism rarely seen nowadays, but her demeanor is slipping. She looks unsure.

There's a knock at the door before it cracks open. "Mr. Grant's lawyer is here," the officer announces.

Fuckface sighs, but my eyes remain locked with Grace's. "Let him in."

Walking into the room, Earl Jenkins informs Grace and Fuckface, "I'll need thirty minutes with my client." God love Earl. He's been the lawyer for this club for years now, always running to our rescue when one of us finds ourselves on the wrong side of the law. And he's got Fuckface stuck between a rock and a hard place with nowhere to go.

Fuckboy glares at me before finally shoving away from the table and moving toward the door. Grace bows her head in disappointment, but also gets up and follows him out of the room.

I look up at Earl. "Please tell me the guys found my kids."

Earl claps a hand on my shoulder. "They're good," he assures me. "Hashtag found them at his place with his kid."

Of course he did. Kevin wouldn't go anywhere

without Hashtag's daughter, Hayden. The anxiety that had been brimming over the surface disappears almost entirely at this news.

"Good," I reply. "Now, how the fuck are you gonna get me outta here?"

Chapter 17

Grace

AFTER THE LAST FEW DAYS, a quiet evening at home in my favorite yoga pants is just the thing I need to clear my head. And a glass of wine. A big one. Maybe the entire bottle.

I have never been this conflicted about a case at any point in my professional career. I've been forced to sit back and watch as the justice system pulls families apart, one right after another. But in this case, I just don't know what to do with it. It's all piling on top of me, pulling me in opposite directions. Now with the kids missing, it's all imploding.

Tyson Jackson.

Eugene Grant.

The Tucker kids.

My boss.

Aaron.

Well, for the latter, that's done. But Eugene Grant? I don't even know how to unpack all the baggage with him. He's a dangerous man with dangerous friends, but his care of Natalie and Kevin is out of left field from what little I know about him. His eyes never strayed from mine as Aaron attempted to grill him about the kids and their missing uncle. Aaron was so focused on his club affiliation, he never noticed the softness in his eyes when he talked about the kids. He loves them, I'm sure of that, but their father is out there.

Legally, the father has the stronger case. Though, if it weren't my case, I don't think I'd agree with the courts after seeing his background check. He's been to jail. I'd have made the case that he had been rehabilitated, but the pending assault charge at the bottom of the report tells me otherwise. Putting those kids into his custody would only ensure they would spend the rest of their lives in a broken, unsettled home. I can't let that happen. But how can I stand in front of a judge and demand that someone with no blood ties is the better match than a blood relative?

*What am I going to do?*

My head falls onto my hand when a knock sounds at

the door. Shifting off of my couch, I grab my wallet from the kitchen bar top when I pass before opening the door.

"Must be a slow night. I didn't expect you so soon," I mumble, shuffling through my wallet for a couple of tens. When I look up, a pair of dark eyes stare down at me. My jaw drops in shock. Eugene Grant is here. At my house.

"We need to talk."

"How did you find out where I live?" My voice shakes, but somehow, I don't think it's from fear. He smirks when he notices.

"I know a guy. Can I come in?"

"You're here alone?"

"My club doesn't follow me like lost sheep, Grace." The way he says my name sends a shiver down my spine. Half excitement, half confusion. "I want to talk to you about Kevin and Natalie. In private."

"Do you know where they are?"

"We'll get to that." If he's here, he has to know where they are. If they were still missing, there's not a doubt in my mind he'd be out there looking for them.

I step back and wave him inside. His boots thump heavily on the floor while I close the door behind us. Alone. In my house. *Please, don't let this be a mistake.*

He turns in a circle. "Nice place. Suits you."

"What's that supposed to mean?"

"The style of the place. It's a little rough around the

edges, but a classic beauty." I blink. Is he hitting on me? He steps closer, nearly pinning me between the door and his body, the smell of his woodsy cologne filling the surrounding air. "I like your hair when it's down."

"You said you wanted to talk about Kevin and Natalie." I force down the lump in my throat. His closeness sets me on edge. His compliments even more so. In a good way, I think. Too good.

"I do."

I try to deflect. "Why don't we sit down, then?" Sliding out from between the door and his body, I walk over to the couch. Eugene follows me closely, and when he sits down, the springs creak under his frame. He shifts a few times before finally settling.

"Sorry. My furniture isn't really built for a big guy like you."

He laughs. "Most aren't."

I reach for a notebook on the coffee table, but his large hand reaches out to stop me, the roughness of his skin caressing mine.

"This has to be off the record."

"Okay," I respond, pulling away from his touch.

He takes a deep breath. "My club saved Kevin and Natalie from a sex trafficking ring a few months ago."

The world around me stills as his words sink in.

"One of my guys found out a local trafficking ring

had taken his daughter, and we traced her kidnapping back to Kevin."

"Kevin... he did that?" How could a boy his age be involved in such a thing? He's barely a teenager. It can't be true.

"He didn't have a choice. It was the uncle, the one reported missing. The one your little cop friend grilled me about yesterday? He took in the kids when their mom died. Turns out, he was a sex trafficker, and saw a prime new candidate in Natalie. Randall made Kevin a deal, that if he brought him new girls, he wouldn't sell her."

My hand flies to my mouth. "Oh my God!"

"He did it, and his last target was the daughter of one of my men. We tracked them down and rescued her and the kids."

"What about their uncle, Randall? You told the police you didn't know anything about him."

"He won't be bothering the kids anymore."

"You mean, you..."

"He's not a threat."

He killed him. There's not a doubt in my mind. The Black Hoods rescued the kids and took him out like yesterday's trash on dumpster day. Justifiable as it was, it's still murder. There's a murderer on my couch. A flipping killer. Aaron was right.

"That's why they're with you."

"Yes. They needed a safe place to recover, and I had an empty house with no one in it."

"I don't understand. Why would you want to take on two kids in, well, your line of work, I guess you could call it?"

"I was a dad for just a short while before I lost my son. I've been alone for a long time, and Kevin and Natalie need someone who will protect them. I want to give them a good life, a happy life. One where they don't have to worry that someone is going to rip them away again." His honesty shines through his dark eyes, like he's giving me a piece of his soul.

Why is he telling me this now? Why tell me about his club's dealings with the trafficking ring? I'm an outsider to their world. An outsider who has the authority to take those kids away from him.

"Why didn't you call the police?"

His eyes narrow. "I think you know why. All I care about is that they're safe, and they were until DFPS got involved."

"You mean, me."

"Yes. I know you're just doing your job, but these kids are fine with me. They're happy. I can give them the life they deserve with a big family that loves them."

"By family, you mean your club. A group of violent vigilantes."

His body stiffens before I get the last word out.

"If that's what you want to call my club, sure. But we do what the police won't. We protect our own, and those who can't protect themselves. So, if you want to label us vigilantes, have at it. It doesn't change a fucking thing." His voice is almost a growl.

"It's illegal."

"There's a lot of illegal things that happen every single day, but you don't see those people trying to clean up the streets or save three innocent kids from a life of abuse, do you? Surely you can understand that."

"I do, and I don't. I'm bound by the law to protect children. You're lawless. You do as you please without consequences."

"There are plenty of consequences, Grace. It's just not us who has to pay the ferryman."

"So what happens to Kevin and Natalie when your club gets mixed up in something, putting them in the crosshairs?"

His face changes. "It'll never happen," he states matter-of-factly. "Those kids will never be in harm's way."

"You can't guarantee that. You know you can't. I know you think you can provide a great life for those kids, but there's always going to be someone out there who wants revenge for something your club did. They'll be the ones who are hurt in the end."

"They won't. When you love two people as much as I love those kids, I'd put myself in the line of fire to protect them, and so would my club. They're a part of us now. If you'd give me a chance, you'd see that too."

"I can't just give chances away like that. The courts decide the cases, and I just investigate them. I have no power."

"You have more power than you think."

If he only knew the truth. I'm powerless. I always have been. Helping kids is all I've wanted to do, but I'm not a judge. I'm not an attorney. I'm the bad guy who rips families apart, along with my own heart.

"Do you trust me?" he asks.

I blink, unsure of how to answer. Finally, I decide that in this case, honesty is the best policy. "I don't know how I could."

"Just try. I need you to come with me."

"You want me to come with you, right now? At this hour?"

"Yes. I need you to understand what I'm trying to tell you. The only way you can do that is to come with me."

I consider his proposal. Riding off into the night with this man isn't smart, but there's something about his honesty that makes a part of me feel safe around him. I've always been on the hunt for the answers in my cases and going with him may be my only shot at finding Natalie and Kevin. With a deep sigh, I send up a silent prayer.

"I'll get my jacket."

Chapter 18

## Judge

"I'M NOT GETTING ON THAT," she says as I hand her my helmet. "I'll just take my car and follow you."

Laughing, I place it on her head. "You'll love it. Might even loosen you up a little."

The helmet sits on top of her bun, making it look uncomfortable. Lifting it off, she holds it under one arm and uses the other to pull out one hairpin after another, letting it fall around her shoulders in long, loose curls.

As I watch her run her fingers through them, I have to force myself to remain cool. Her hair smells fruity and fresh. Though I wouldn't normally think of fruity as a sexy scent, coming from her, it most definitely is. Grace is a looker, even with that tight ass bun. But her hair curling around her shoulders makes her look like a fucking angel.

"There." With a self-conscious smirk, she puts the helmet back on. I still can't move. All I can do is watch her fingers work at the strap beneath her chin and wonder how I never noticed before just how good she smells.

Shifting on her feet, she arches her brow. "Is something wrong?"

I blink, clearing my mind of wanting to press my nose into her neck and breathing in her scent. "Nah, we're good," I say as I climb onto my motorcycle. I start it up, bringing the roaring engine to life before turning to Grace. "Hop on!"

Sinking her teeth into her bottom lip, she looks at the seat behind me. Her lips move, as if she's mumbling to herself. Then finally, she nods and places her hands on my shoulders as she swings her leg over the seat.

It's been a long fucking time since I've had a woman on the seat behind me, and none of them had ever molded to me as perfectly as Grace's tiny form does. Her breasts press against my back as her thighs settle along either side of my hips, allowing me to feel her heat.

*Jesus, Judge. You need to get laid. And fast.*

The ride to the clubhouse takes about fifteen minutes. Kevin and Natalie are outside with GP's old lady, Blair, and their dog, Walter. They all pause in their game of fetch and watch as I back my motorcycle at the front of the line, their faces frozen in shock.

Kevin's face twists in confusion. And maybe even betrayal. "What's she doing here?" he asks.

Taking Grace's hand, I help her off the seat. Her cheeks are pink from the ride, and her hair is wild beneath the helmet.

Once she's on her feet, I take her hand, completely ignoring how soft her skin is, and lead her toward the kids.

Walter, likely sensing the tension in the air, presses against Blair's leg and growls. Walter was a rescue from a dog fighting ring last year, and his looks are the scariest part of him. He doesn't trust easily, but he'll defend who he loves to the death.

"Why is she here?" Kevin asks again.

I hold up a hand to stop him. "Relax, bud. I brought her here to talk. To talk to all of us. Thought maybe we could tell her our story."

Kevin glares at us both. "No. I'm not telling this bitch anything. Come on, Nat." Grabbing his sister's hand, he goes to drag her away.

"Kevin," I bark out, stopping him in his tracks. "I know you're trying to protect your sister, but you gotta trust me on this. Let me protect the both of you."

"Kevin?" Grace calls. "I promise you, whatever you tell me tonight will stay between us."

"Bullshit."

"Hey!" I know he's feeling betrayed, but I don't like the way he's talking to Grace.

"It's okay," Grace says, placing her soft hand on my arm as she focuses on Kevin. "I was an orphan too," she tells him. "I've been through a lot. I could tell you stories that would keep you up at night. And when I became a social worker, it was to help kids like me—kids like the both of you—and make sure none of them had to go through any of the stuff I did."

None of us speak. All of us—even Walter—are staring at Grace. As prim and proper as she might seem, I'd never once stopped to consider how she'd gotten to be that way. I'd never thought about her past or her history, or what made her hide herself behind a pencil skirt and an old-school marm hairdo.

"If we talk to you, do you promise not to take us away from Mr. Judge?" Natalie asks, pulling her hand from her brother's to stand beside me.

Grace turns to her, giving her a smile that melts me a little inside. "I promise, honey. I just want to know what's going on, and to make sure you and your brother are safe."

Natalie stares at her for a long moment, and then nods. Taking Grace's hand, she leads her to the closest picnic table. Once they're both seated, Kevin grumbles something under his breath before taking a seat across from them.

"What do you want to know?" Natalie asks, her enormous eyes filled with hope.

"Everything," Grace replies, looking to Kevin. "Start from the beginning."

Kevin's shoulders slump in defeat, and his defiant attitude fades away. "The beginning sucks."

Grace smiles sadly. "I'm sure it does. Why don't you tell me about it?"

Kevin looks to me, and I nod, giving him permission to tell her.

Sighing, he digs his fingernail into a groove on the table, sliding it back and forth, making the groove a little deeper with each shallow pass. "Our momma wasn't a very good one," he tells her. "She drank a lot. She had men over all the time, and they would make us go in the bedroom so they could do drugs and stuff."

"Did those men ever touch either of you?"

Kevin shakes his head. "No. A couple of them wanted to, but Momma threatened to hurt them if they tried."

Grace nods, but says nothing.

"One day, when Nat was eight, and I was twelve, she said she had something to do. She told us she'd be back in an hour, but she never came back. We found out later that she died."

Kevin's knee bounces as he tells the story, and he doesn't make eye contact with any of us. Instead, he stares off into the distance as he speaks.

"They didn't even tell us how she died. My uncle just showed up one day and told us the police had been to see him. They told him Momma was dead, and that we had to go live with him now."

"And how did you feel about that?" Grace asks.

Kevin's jaw tightens. "Momma hated Uncle Randall. Said he was a pervert. We didn't really know him at all."

She turns her attention to Natalie. "And how did you feel while all of this was going on?"

Natalie shrugs. "I was just little. I mean, I was only eight years old. I just knew that Kevin would take care of me, so as long as we were together, I'd be okay."

Blair looks at me from across the table. She knows as well as I do what went on at Uncle Randall's house.

"So how was it living with your uncle?"

"He was a pervert," Kevin bites out. "He kidnapped little girls and kept them in his basement. Gross smelling older men came over every night and gave him money to be alone with those girls. And then someone would come and get them to take them somewhere else, and he would kidnap a couple more."

Grace swallows. "Did he…" She clears her throat. "Did he make you guys go into that basement?"

"He took Natalie down there every night, but he never sold her. We had a deal. I would bring him new girls whenever he needed them, and he wouldn't let any of those men do anything but look at my sister."

A tear slides down Grace's cheek, but she doesn't give any other indication of her own heartbreak. "That must have been incredibly scary."

Natalie wraps her arms around herself as she trembles. In that moment, I wish I could bring Randall back from the dead so I could wring his fucking neck and kill him all over again, just for making my girl feel this way.

"That's how we got to be with Gene," Kevin continues. "He saved us and took us in. He bought us new clothes and gave us the nicest home we've ever had. Everything with him is amazing." He eyeballs Grace. "Until you came along."

A heart-wrenching sob rips through Natalie's throat. "Please, don't take us away. I want to stay with Mr. Judge. He keeps us safe. We need him, and he needs us."

Grace's tear-stained face turns to me and our eyes meet. For the first time since she stormed into that bar with a giant stick up her ass, I feel relief. She gets it. She finally gets it.

## Grace

DINNER. *Why did I agree to dinner at his place?* I rub my hand over my face in frustration. I shouldn't be doing this, seeing him again. Seeing the kids who are still classified as runaways. Yet here I am, on my way to his house to see what life is like under his roof. What is it about this man that seems to draw me into his life when it only complicates mine? He makes me question everything. My sanity. My job. My morality. Nothing is safe when it comes to Eugene Grant.

A horn blasts from behind me. *Shit. How long has the light been green?* With a polite wave to the person behind me, I press my foot on the gas pedal and drive until his house comes into view. It's a small home nestled up on a small street with a few older homes on either side. His Harley is parked in the driveway near a large pickup truck. The white siding stands out against the more historic homes surrounding it.

An older man stares at me as I pull into the drive and exit my car.

"Evening," I greet him with a wave, and he waves back politely.

I knock on the door a few times, but no one responds. *Odd.* I try the doorbell, and that's when I hear running footsteps barreling toward the door. When the door opens, I find Natalie's face beaming up at me.

"Miss Grace. You're here!" she chirps excitedly.

"Hi, Natalie."

"Come on in. Dinner's almost ready."

Stepping through the door, my eyes grow wide. His home is neat, with little decoration outside of the essentials. A large, black leather couch takes up most of the front room, facing a flat screen television on the opposite wall. A few books lie stacked on the end table next to it. Kevin sits on the couch with a game controller in his hand.

"Kevin, looks who's here."

"I know who she is, Natalie," he retorts, his attention on the game.

Grabbing my hand, she leads me through the room and into a mid-size kitchen. Eugene's back is to me as he stirs something on the stove.

"She's here, Mr. Judge," Natalie announces once more. He turns, and my mouth falls open. Around his waist is a bright pink apron with cats all over it. A slow smile spreads across my lips as I look him up and down.

"Nice apron," I giggle, making him laugh.

"It came with the house," he jokes. "Hope you're not hungry."

"I'm starving."

"I apologize in advance, then. I'm not the best cook."

Smiling, I offer, "I'm sure it will be fine."

Natalie tugs at my hand and pulls me to a table near the back of the kitchen. After I take a seat, she settles into the one next to me. Eugene, clutching a pan of food with matching bright pink pot holders, sets it down in the middle of the table. The smell is intoxicating. He's obviously better in the kitchen than he lets on.

"Kevin!" he yells out. "Food!"

Kevin comes in from the front room and plops down into the seat at the farthest end of the table. Training his eyes on me, he watches my every move as Natalie yaps away next to me. Joining us, Eugene reaches out for my plate, fills it with servings from each dish, then hands it back to me. When I look at the food, it takes everything I have not to drool on it. Mashed potatoes, country gravy, green beans, and a steak that takes up over half the plate. I have a good appetite, but

I don't think I've ever seen this much food outside of the buffet line.

"Thank you. It looks great."

I try to focus on the meal and the conversations at hand, but my gaze continues to shift over to Kevin. He's not eating, just pushing the food around on his plate as if something's on his mind.

"You okay, bud?" Eugene asks when he notices.

"Yeah," Kevin replies. "I'm not hungry. Can I be excused?"

"Sure."

Taking his plate to the refrigerator, he places it inside before leaving the room. I hear footsteps as he ascends to the second floor.

"He's mad at you," Natalie mutters. "He thinks you're going to take us away from Mr. Judge. I tried to tell him you wouldn't, but he doesn't believe me."

My heart sinks. Kevin's been in the system so long, he understands what my job entails, and knows what I do to families like this. I'm an outsider, someone who can ruin the good thing they've got going here. Am I capable of his worst fears? Am I really going to break up yet another happy family because Eugene doesn't share an ounce of blood with these kids? I look over to Eugene, who stops chewing mid-bite. My lips thin as I try to think of a way to answer her.

We eat in silence a few minutes longer, until Natalie pushes her plate away with a satisfied smile on her face. "Do you know anything about make-up?" she asks, her question coming out of left field. "I'm trying to learn how to do that whole cat-eye thing, but I can't figure it out."

"Um, kinda? I'm no professional, but I know a thing or two."

Judge shakes his head. "You have homework, kiddo."

Her smile turns to a frown. "I know. Maybe later?"

"Tell you what. You get your homework done, and I'll see what I can do."

"Promise?"

"Of course." I beam at her, marking an X over my chest. "Cross my heart."

Happy with that, she shoves away from the table, gives us both a wave, and then follows the same path her brother took.

"Eugene—" I start, just as my cell phone rings. Retrieving it, I see my supervisor's name on the screen.

"I'm sorry, but I have to take this." Getting to my feet, I head back into the living room and answer the call.

"Hello?"

"Where are you?" Eric snaps. "I need an update on the Tucker case. It's been days since they approved the removal order."

"I'm taking some comp time, but I assure you, I'm

still working on the case." In a sense. If he knew where I was right now, he'd lose it.

"You're still working on it? Grace, do your job."

"I am doing my job, Eric. I couldn't have predicted the kids would take off when we tried to execute the order. Had the police not been so hell-bent on escalating the situation with Mr. Grant, we would've had them by now."

A white lie if I ever told one. Pushing the blame back on Aaron seems harsh, but it's true. His insistence on stepping into the middle of their club caused a ruckus, but I can't reveal that I know where the kids are just yet, especially with not having all the cards out on the table with their case. The real cards. Not the ones the courts have on paper.

"I want results, Halfpenny. Find them." The line goes dead, and I turn to find a fuming Eugene behind me.

"How much did you hear?" I ask nervously.

"Enough," he growls.

"It's not what it seems."

He takes a few steps toward me, the mom chic apron he had on earlier gone. His tight black shirt sticks to his torso like glue, highlighting his muscles. I look at the bulging vein at his temple as he stops short of crashing into me.

"After everything I've told you, what the kids have

told you, you still want to take them away from me, don't you?"

I've never been on this side of his rage, and it takes a mere two seconds to understand how he can command such a large motorcycle club with one glare. He's intimidating, but my body responds unexpectedly as my core ignites.

"It's my job, Eugene. You know that."

He presses his index finger against my breastbone. "I had hoped that somewhere in this chest of yours, you had a heart."

"My heart breaks every fucking time I have to take part in ripping a family to shreds," I bite out. "I barely sleep at night because all I see are their faces when I close my eyes. I hear their screams as they cry out for their parents or guardians."

"Break the cycle," he challenges. "Walk away from the case and leave these kids with me."

I shake my head. "I can't. If I don't, someone else will come."

"These kids fucking belong to me. You can't come into my house and make all these promises you know you can't keep." I can feel his hot, heavy breath cascade over me.

"I know that!" I scream, the truth finally spilling from my lips. "Don't you think I know that? If I had a magic wand, I would just wave it and give you custody, but I don't. Their criminal father has legal rights in the eyes of the court."

That gets his attention. "Criminal?"

"When I called to talk to him about his missing persons report, I requested a background check on him. He has a rap sheet a mile long. Possession. Intent to sell. Breaking and entering. Pending charges for assault. He's not a good person."

"That it? I can handle their father."

"How? By making him disappear like you did with their uncle? Murder is not the answer. You can't just kill anyone who opposes you." The words feel foreign leaving my lips, and he doesn't flinch once. For a normal person, this would sound absurd. For Eugene, though, it's probably everyday decisions, and I don't know how I feel about that.

"That's how you see me? A savage bastard with blood on his hands? I'm not the boogeyman underneath your bed, Grace."

"Then what are you?"

He prowls toward me, his eyes still filled with anger. A smart person would back away, but maybe I'm not as smart as I think I am, because as he gets closer, I can only stand there, frozen in place.

Placing his hands on my hips, he walks me back until

I'm pressed against the wall. His breath fans across my face as he glowers down at me. "Why are you so goddamn infuriating?"

I arch against him, shocking us both. His chest is hard against mine, and now my nose is mere inches from his. Panting, we stare into each other's angry eyes.

"Why are you such a brute?" We continue to stare at each other, our gazes imprisoned in the fire burning between us, the anger morphing into something far different.

When his lips crash onto mine, I lose myself. My fingertips dig into his shoulders and pull him impossibly closer. Whimpering into his mouth, I raise up on my toes, trying to put as much of him against me as humanly possible.

*Holy Mother of God.* The contrast between his soft lips and his rough beard makes my knees quake beneath me, threatening to fail me altogether.

His kiss carries me outside of myself. Away from my job, my past. Away from everything but the fact that I'm a woman, and this is the first man to ever make me feel this kind of passion.

Time stands still as he presses me against that wall. He pulls me closer, his fingers curling into my hips, sending a steady buzz of heady excitement all throughout my body.

"Uh, Mr. Judge?"

His lips pause, and for a moment, we stay that way, needing a second to compose ourselves and remember our surroundings.

When he finally pulls away, I'm able to get a view of Natalie standing in the doorway, her eyes wide with confusion, her body trembling.

Eugene moves to her in an instant, his thumbs wiping away her tears as they fall. "What's wrong, honey?"

Deciding she doesn't care as much about what she just walked in on nearly as much as what brought her here in the first place, she shouts, "Kevin's being a big fat jerk!"

"Come here, sugar." Opening his arms, she throws herself into him. "What did he say to you?"

"I was trying to work on my spelling and I needed a little help, so I asked him. He just told me to get lost."

"I'll take care of it, Natty Kat. Why don't you go get your homework, and maybe Miss Grace will help you with it?" He looks over his shoulder, and I nod.

She smiles up at me. "Really?"

"Of course I will."

Pushing away from Eugene, she runs back into the living room, and I hear her taunting her brother about how much trouble he's in.

Running back in with her book, she takes me by the

hand and drags me to the kitchen table. Eugene watches us for a few minutes before heading into what I assume is a hard conversation with Kevin about his behavior. Turning my attention back to Natalie, she reads a few pages and stops, repeating a sentence over and over again.

"See!" she exclaims. "How can the word there mean three different things? It's so confusing."

I chuckle. There are grown adults who don't know the difference between their, there, and they're. "Their means belongs to them. They're means they are. And there means the opposite of here. Like, over there."

She wrinkles her nose. "That's still confusing."

She's right. It is confusing. "Um... Let's try them in sentences and see if you can figure out the right version of each word."

I watch as she writes out the sentences in scribbled handwriting, and for the first time, I realize that for a child her age, she's extremely far behind in reading, and God knows what else. She's going to struggle unnecessarily thanks to her upbringing.

A noise draws my attention to the doorway where Eugene waves me over.

"Keep going. I'll be right back," I tell her, pointing at the page.

Slipping from the chair, I walk over to him. His face is nearly unreadable.

"I have to go take care of something."

"Oh, I can go if you need me to leave."

"That's not what I'm asking, Grace. I know I have no right to ask, but can you stay here with the kids?"

"You're putting that much trust in me?" It wasn't too long ago that I was here to remove the kids. Now he wants to leave them alone with me?

"You're already here, and my niece Lindsey is at her night class. It would save me a lot of time if you could."

I really shouldn't be considering it, but his eyes are begging me to accept. It would be nice to be alone with the kids again. Without his influence around, I might connect with Kevin.

I give in. "Sure."

"It shouldn't be long. I normally send the kids to bed around nine, but Kevin's already in his room. If he gives you any trouble, remind him of our little talk." He gives me a wink. "Nat, I have to leave for a bit. You be good for Miss Grace."

"You mean you're staying the night?" she asks, her eyes wide. "Can we have a sleepover? I've always wanted to have one."

"I can't stay the night—"

"Of course she will," Eugene answers for me without

145

looking in my direction. He's smarter than he looks. "I'll just leave you two ladies to have your fun. I'll be back as soon as I can."

Grabbing his keys and cut from the counter, and heads out the back door. The second it shuts, Natalie gives me a mischievous look.

"Do you like scary movies?"

What did I just agree to?

## Judge

GRACE, with a tight bun and serious expression, is a beautiful woman. Watching her sleep on my couch with her hair all over the place is breathtaking. She's stretched out on her back, with one foot resting on the floor. Her mouth is open just a little, but she's taken her hair down, the loose curls flowing around her sleeping face.

It's almost two o'clock in the morning though, and there's no way she's spending the night on this lumpy ass couch. "Grace," I whisper, nudging her shoulder.

Nothing.

"Grace." This time, I say it a little louder, shaking her shoulder.

Still, nothing.

"Darlin', either you wake up, or I'll carry your ass up to bed. Your choice."

Her forehead wrinkles with a frown before her eyelids flutter open. She blinks up at me and her frown deepens. "I'm not getting in your bed."

She sits up, turning to right herself on the couch, which puts her on the opposite end from where I stand. "Did you just get home?"

I nod. "Alarm went off at a garage we just bought. Nobody there, but a window was broken, so we stuck around to board it up."

"Who would do that?"

I chuckle. "The Black Hoods have a lot of friends out there, sweetheart, but we have a lot who don't like us much too. Could've been someone who has a beef with us. Could've been some punk kids causing shit. We'll find out."

She opens her mouth as if to say something, but seems to think better of it. Pushing to her feet, she grabs her jacket and purse off the chair beside her.

"Well, I should get going. It's late."

Of course she should. It makes sense that she does. So why do I not want her to leave? "Stay," I tell her. "Natalie thinks you're spending the night. She'll be looking for you when she wakes up."

Grace gapes at me, that frown reappearing on her forehead. "I can't sleep here. It wouldn't be right."

"I can't let you go home at this time of night

unescorted. That wouldn't be right."

Curling her hand into a fist, she props it on her hip. "You're such a frustrating man."

"So?"

I can't help it. I shouldn't be goading her, but her hair's a mess, her clothes are disheveled, and her cheeks are still pink from sleep. She looks adorable.

"Goodnight, Eugene." Pushing past me, she moves toward the front door.

"What about the kids?" I ask as she walks away. "What are you going to do with our case?"

Pausing, she turns. Placing her jacket and purse on a nearby bench, she comes back to sit on the couch. "Honestly, I don't know."

What the fuck does she mean, she doesn't know? "Were you not paying attention when the kids told you their history?"

She purses her lips. "Of course I did."

"Did you not see how settled in they are here? This is their fucking home, Grace."

"I know it is. I saw and heard everything you and the kids said and did, and it means the world to me that the three of you trusted me enough to let me in on the truth of your situation. Not many men in your position would do that, I don't think."

She's right. People who live the MC lifestyle are

usually a different breed. They don't follow the same rules as everyone else. They don't rely on anyone but the people in their club when they need something. And they never go to the authorities. Not for anything.

And in the grand scheme of things, when it comes to these kids, Grace *is* the authorities. She has the power to allow me to keep them.

"Have a seat," she says, indicating the chair across from her.

I stare at her for a moment, unaccustomed to being told what to do in my own damn house. But I do it, curious as to what she's going to say.

"Henry Tucker is a dangerous man, Eugene. I mean, really terrible." She shivers. "I don't just mean the stuff in his file, either. I can just feel it in my soul. He can't get his hands on Kevin and Natalie."

Finally, something we can agree on.

"So, what are you going to do?"

"Honestly, my hands are tied here. Their father has legal rights to them. The judges always rule in favor of the biological parent, and I don't see why this case would be any different."

My jaw aches as she speaks, and I have to force myself to relax it.

"There's no way in hell they'll ever go with that man. Even if I end up spending twenty-five to life in prison for ripping his throat out with my bare hands, Kevin and Natalie will never end up with him."

Grace shivers again, and I reach behind her, pulling the fleece blanket down from the back of the couch. Unfolding it, I give it a shake and drape it over her shoulders.

"The only thing I can think of," she continues, "is for you to apply to become their legal foster parent. That takes a lot of time, and the review process alone can take weeks. Plus, you'd have to attend classes, and DCS will have free rein over the way you run your home for as long as the kids live here. I have a friend who processes the applications. I could call in a favor."

I chew on that for a moment. "I have a better idea."

Her face brightens a little.

"You give me everything you know about that fucker who claims to be their father. You give me any details that will help us get the cops off our backs. The club will find their father. He'll sign those kids over to me, legally, and then he'll disappear."

Grace is on her feet in an instant, pacing the floor. "I will not take any part in you and your club killing anybody, Eugene Grant. Not even a bad person like him."

Before she can finish the last word, I'm in front of her. Taking her face in my hands, I run the pads of my thumbs along her cheekbones. "I'm not in the business of just offing people, Grace. I'm flattered you think I'm that cold-blooded, but it's just not the way the Black Hoods run things. Not unless we have no other choice."

She doesn't know it, but when our bodies are this close together, her pupils dilate, and her body leans closer, her breasts brushing my chest just enough to count.

"You promise you won't hurt him?"

"Not unless we have no other choice."

I watch as her eyes fall closed, looking as if she's fighting a war inside her mind. Finally, after a few moments, she nods. Her eyes are still closed, but she nods. "Fine. I'll tell you everything. I'll give you the file. Do what you want with it, but I'll need it back the same day."

She looks defeated, while I feel like I've just climbed Mount-fucking-Everest.

I crash my mouth onto hers, her lips soft as they dance against mine, her tongue darting out to glide across my lower lip.

The smell of her hair fills my nose as her body presses even closer to mine. When she moans softly into my mouth, I realize that just being here with her like this silences everything. All the bullshit that invades our minds every day. Bills we need to pay, conversations we could have been cleverer in. What's making that sound on my motorcycle when I rev it up. All of it, gone.

Grace clings to me as I walk her back, only stopping when her ass hits the edge of my kitchen table. Lifting her, I set her on the table and drop to my knees in front of her. Thank the good Lord for pencil skirts. Pushing the skirt up, I expose her long, creamy thighs, and a pair of black lace panties that are begging to be ripped off and done away with.

"It's been a long time since I've been with a man," she whispers. I don't know why she feels the need to tell me this. I don't want to think about Grace being with any man. As far as I'm concerned, she's sitting here in front of me as pure as the driven fucking snow.

"Look at me," I order, waiting for her to meet my gaze. "Watch me."

She pants, and her body trembles as I reach my finger forward, hooking the tiny piece of lace that covers her most intimate area.

Placing my finger on her clit, I look up to see her eyes roll back as I move the tiny bundle of nerves with my finger. She parts her lips, her breaths coming fast.

"Do you want me to fuck you, Grace?" I press harder, my own excitement jutting against the inside of my jeans.

"Yes." Sitting up a little, she yanks my shirt up and over my head before fumbling with my buckle, but I stop her. Placing a hand on her chest, I gently push her back until she's splayed out in front of me like a Thanksgiving Day feast. "Please."

"Please what, baby?" I ask, drawing slow, lazy circles over her clit, loving the wanton way she rolls her hips.

"Fuck me."

She doesn't have to ask me twice. I wasn't kidding when I'd said it had been a while. It's been well over a year at this point.

Reaching down, I fumble with my pants until I'm free, my cock heavy and long, and hard as a rock.

It only takes a moment to place my head at her entrance, and then I'm inside of her. And it feels like fucking heaven.

Together we move, and her body arches and twists from side to side, her breasts on full display. As I drive myself into her, I lean forward, nipping and licking at her rock-hard nipples as they bounce just inches from my face.

Her body shudders as she comes for me. On me. The walls of her sex surrounding me. I watch in awe as a flush spreads across her cheeks, and another across her chest. And then she's tightening around me, falling apart around me, and falling apart again.

And then, just when I think I can't take another

minute of it, I fall with her, consumed by the pleasure rushing through my entire body as I stare into her eyes.

"You're incredible," I whisper, leaning forward to press against her, even though we're still locked together in the most romantic and odd pairing I've ever seen. "You're a fucking miracle."

## Chapter 21

Grace

"COULDN'T we have taken your truck?" I grumble as I dismount his motorcycle. It's kind of hard to get on and off one of those beasts in a pencil skirt without showing off a little more than people need to see. And considering we're right outside the coffee shop I go to every morning, and being that coffee shop is right next to my office, I'd rather not show off anything I don't normally show.

Eugene just grins as he helps me unhook the helmet. Once he's done, he leans in close and whispers, "Maybe I like the way you feel against me on my bike."

Goose bumps race along my arms, and my belly dips a little. "That so?"

"What can I say? I'm a gentleman."

"Well, Mr. Gentleman, you've delivered me safely to work. I think I can handle it the rest of the way."

"What kind of gentleman would I be if I didn't make sure you got safely inside?"

"The kind of gentleman I shouldn't be seen with, considering I'm working a case with two children in your care."

He knows I'm right. This morning, I'd argued with him until I was blue in my face over how I didn't need him to escort me to work. But when my car wouldn't start, I had no other choice. One unscheduled day off may have gone overlooked by my boss, but two in a row, he'd be suspicious. I had to make an appearance.

"Go get your coffee, and when you're inside your building, I'll leave."

"Does that caveman thing work on all the women in your life?"

"I think my kitchen table would attest that it does." He smiles again, his gaze never leaving mine as he pulls me closer to him. His lips graze against my ear. "Can't wait to show you what I can do in my bed."

My face instantly flushes. We're in public, and he talks about us sleeping together again like it's no big deal. It's a huge deal. I'm effectively sleeping with the enemy, and he wants to flaunt that fact right here on the street. Pushing away from him gently, I frown.

"What time do you get off?" The way he says that simple phrase makes it sound dirty.

"I should be done around five."

"I'll meet you here."

"That won't work," I inform him. "I have a date tonight."

Jealousy hardens his features. "A date?"

"I guess you could come with me."

"You want me to come with you on this date?"

"Trust me," I say with a grin. "Oh, and bring the truck. We'll have to grab him dinner before we go."

His frown turns into a laugh, making my heart soar. "You have strange dates."

I shrug. "When you meet Greg, you'll understand."

Chuckling, he pats my behind. "Just get your coffee."

I smile all the way into the coffee shop. Thankfully, at this hour, the lines are generally short, and today is no exception. My normal barista, Katie, stands behind the counter and waves when she spots me coming through the door. Her short blonde bob is now a bright shade of green.

"Good morning," she greets me. "The usual?"

"Of course. And can you throw in three apple turnovers?" The kids were still in bed when we left, and a breakfast surprise may go a long way in helping Kevin's mistrust in me. I hope so, anyway.

"You got it."

Fluttering around the small space, she deposits a bag

alongside my coffee on the counter. Using the gift card Eric had given me for my birthday last month, I pay Katie and give her a three-dollar tip. Then, grabbing my purchases, I head over to the side counter for a couple of packets of sweetener. That's when an uneasy feeling rushes over me.

Turning, I freeze when I see a strange, disheveled, angry man moving toward me.

"Where are my kids?" he growls.

"I'm sorry?" I ask, trying to keep my voice even. My eyes dart around the store, but besides the baristas busy behind the counter, I'm all alone with him. "I don't know what you're talking about."

"Bullshit," he spits. And I mean, he literally spits. Everything about him is quaking with rage. "I want my fucking kids back."

I try to peer over his shoulder to see if Eugene has a clear view of me, but the man snaps his fingers just an inch away from my face.

"Don't you look for your biker boyfriend. He can't help you, anyway."

How could he possibly know about Eugene? Unless... he's been watching us?

"That white trash piece of shit has my kids, and you're letting him keep them."

*Oh my God.* Henry Tucker looks much different from

the mugshots in the file Aaron gave me. He looks strung out, scrawny, and like he hasn't showered in a very long time.

"Mr. Tucker, why don't we move this discussion to my office." Where there's an audience. And security guards. "This is not the place to discuss custody issues."

Breathe in, breathe out. *Stay calm, Grace. Remember your training. Defuse the situation and hope he backs off.*

"The fuck it isn't. You bastards have my kids and you're hiding them from me. I know it, and you know it." He pushes up against me, and I feel a firm object being pressed into my side. "You're going to take me to them."

*Holy shit.* My body jolts with terror when I realize just what it is pressed against me. He has a gun. I'm helpless and at his mercy, and he knows it. There's no way out of this unless Eugene takes notice from outside.

"Okay," I whisper. Katie's watching now. She raises her phone and mouths, "9-1-1." I give her the faintest nod I can manage, praying Tucker doesn't see it. "Whatever you say."

"Walk toward the door," he orders. Leaving my coffee and bag, I do as he commands. Digging the gun into my side, he uses it to force me toward a side door I'd never seen before, away from the front door where Eugene sits on his bike. Away from my only chance of escape.

"Keep moving."

He reaches past me for the handle, but it swings wide, and three police officers stand on the other side of it. My eyes meet his, seeing his panic. The object falls away from my side, and I take my chance. I shove myself forward, between the officers and away from Henry. Running at top speed down the short alley, I spill out onto the sidewalk, but I don't slow down. My breathing is ragged as I run toward Eugene, who's off his bike in one quick move when he sees me. Slamming into him, I start to cry.

"Grace? What's wrong?"

"Henry Tucker," I gasp. "He was in there. He knows about you and the kids. He wanted me to take him to them. He had a gun, Eugene."

His body goes still.

"Where is he?"

"He was taking me out the side entrance, but there were some cops standing out there talking. I took my chance and ran. I don't know where he went."

He hugs me, and I feel him reach into his pocket and pull out his phone. Pressing it to his ear, he holds me tighter, not letting me go.

A male voice picks up on the other end of the line, and I barely recognize Eugene's voice when he growls, "Call everyone in now. We have a situation."

## Judge

I LEAD Grace into the clubhouse, my blood still boiling. That son of a bitch is off his fucking rocker, trying to abduct Grace with me just outside the door. It tells me he has no boundaries, that he's more dangerous than we thought. And that he's been watching us.

"You can hang out here," I tell her, pointing to the common area of the clubhouse.

It's not much, really. Just a gigantic room with a bar, a cool as hell jukebox Lindsey had found at an auction, and a pool table. Black leather couches are set up in a couple of spots for folks to relax, and there are a couple of tall pub tables with stools.

And at the moment, it's filled with bikers and women, and a couple of kids, including my own. "This is my family," I tell her. "You're safe here."

She looks around nervously, biting at her lip. "Are you sure? The last time I saw these folks, I kind of unintentionally brought along a SWAT team."

Her worries are definitely warranted. The people in this clubhouse won't trust her easily. They never trust an outsider to begin with, not until they've proven themselves. But after being a part of the authorities dropping in on us unexpectedly... well, let's just say, she's gonna have her work cut out for her to do that.

"You're here with me," I tell her. "They may not like you much yet, but they will be respectful."

Her gray eyes look uncertain, but she doesn't argue.

I lead her to one of the sectionals where Lindsey sits with the kids. "Take care of her, would ya?"

Lindsey looks Grace up and down, then nods. She doesn't smile or say hello.

I plant a kiss on Grace's forehead, and I feel everyone's eyes on us, but not one of them has the balls to question me, which is exactly the way I like it.

"Be back shortly."

Nodding, she takes a seat on the couch, and Natalie's quick to sit right beside her. Thank God for her.

"Let's go, boys," I call out, rounding up the troops so we can get this ball rolling.

Chairs scrape across the floor, and the sounds of several pairs of heavy boots follow me into our meeting room. Taking my seat at the head of the table, I watch as the others pour into the room and settle into their spots.

For the first time in a long time, everyone is here. Mom sits to the left of me, then GP and Stone Face. Karma sits to my right, and then Hashtag and Twat Knot fill out the rest of the table.

My crew back together again.

"So," Twat Knot says with a grin, "what's the stripper doin' here?" Karma moves to swat him, but Hashtag is closer and beats him to it. Twat Knot throws his hands up. "Watch the hair, asshole."

Twat Knot comes by his name honestly. That goddamn man-bun he wears every day really does make him look like a fucking twat. And he's obsessed with his fucking hair.

Hashtag rolls his eyes and lifts his middle finger in response.

"If you don't mind," I drawl, giving them both a flat, unamused stare.

"Sorry, Prez," Hashtag mutters, while Twat Knot rearranges that messy fucking bun on top of his head. Once everyone is paying attention, I begin.

"Kevin and Nat have a father. He's come looking for them and put out a missing persons report for them and their pedophile uncle."

"What's his name?" Hashtag asks, likely already

planning to go digging for info on the internet. If information is stored anywhere in the limitless worldwide web, Hashtag will find it. It's what he does.

"His name is Henry Wayne Tucker, and he's one bad dude. The kids don't really remember him, but he's got priors."

"Don't we all?" GP huffs.

"He tried to abduct Grace at gunpoint this morning." That shuts him up. "I was standing right outside. She was in a coffee shop and he walked right in, shoved a gun into her ribs, and forced her out a side door."

"Fuck," GP mutters.

"He wants my fucking kids. A judge has ordered Grace to remove them from my home and hand them over to their father."

Shocked faces stare back at me.

"She's agreed to hand over everything she has to the club and allow us to track this bastard down before that happens. She agrees the kids need to stay with me. Hash, you speak with her before we leave. Find out everything you can. Leave no stone unturned. We need to find this motherfucker before he hurts somebody."

"You got it."

"The rest of you, stay alert. If he's willing to go after Grace with me on the other side of the door, then he's willing to do just about anything. Dude's a fucking wild-card. Nobody rides alone. Keep your families close, and go nowhere without your piece."

"What's the plan once we find him?" Mom asks from beside me.

"He's gonna sign those kids over to me," I tell him. "And then I'm gonna rip his fucking head off."

Grace

I NEVER THOUGHT I would step foot in this clubhouse again after the failed removal, yet here I am, sitting on a huge leather sectional with Eugene's niece and one of the other guy's girlfriend who I know now is Blair. Kevin and Natalie took off down the hallway with another teenager the second the conference room door shut with Eugene and the rest of the men. Except for a couple of guys who sit near the front door, eyeing me closely.

"Will they be okay?"

"Oh yeah," Lindsey replies. "That's Hayden. She and Kevin are as thick as thieves since the incident."

"She's the daughter who was taken by Randall," I surmise, remembering my earlier conversation with Eugene Kevin's last catfish for his uncle that ended up freeing them all. The reason Kevin and Natalie are living with Eugene.

"She was," Blair acknowledges. "All three of them have been through so much, but I think spending time together has helped them to work through the trauma. Hashtag wasn't so fond of the idea, but it's been the best thing for them."

"Hashtag? Where do you guys come up with these crazy nicknames?"

"It's just a thing bikers do. Some earn them, and some are born with them." Blair laughs. "They all call me Red, thanks to GP."

I grin, admiring her gorgeous head of red, curly hair, and then turn my attention to Lindsey. "Do you have one?"

She smirks. "Not one they'd say to my face if they do."

"Because Karma wouldn't allow it," Blair adds, earning a side-eye from Lindsey, but she doesn't seem to care, keeping her smile firmly in place. Why do I get the feeling they're having a silent conversation about this Karma guy I'm not privy to?

"So, do you all live here?" I ask, changing the subject.

Blair shakes her head. "No. Most of us have our own homes. GP and I live nearby."

"I kind of float around between my uncle's house and

here. It just depends on your situation. Some of the newer guys prefer to live here until they can get settled."

"Oh." I don't know why, but I'd always assumed bikers lived together like one big commune. This is actually the first time I've really gotten to learn what their lives are really like.

"We don't all live here like one big family," Lindsey huffs. "Believe me, none of us needs that much testosterone in our lives."

"God, no," Blair agrees. "GP's bad enough at our house. I don't need the rest of them under one roof. Our house couldn't survive it. Neither could our refrigerator."

"That's something you need to remember, being my uncle's old lady."

"Old what?" I inquire.

"Old lady," Blair says. "When you're with one of the patches, that's what they call you."

I throw up a hand to stop her. "Patches? I'm sorry, but I don't understand."

"Patches are full members," Lindsey explains. "They have the full patches on the back of their cuts." I nod, only somewhat able to wrap my head around what they're telling me. "Their vests. The guys without them are called prospects. They're kind of the probationary members of the club. They work with a patch mentor, and if they do well enough, they'll become a full member someday."

"And the other women I've seen around here? Are they... what was the word you used... old ladies?"

Lindsey's hands fly up in the air. "Oh, hell no." She points to a small group of women sitting at the bar across the room. "They're what we like to call sweet butts. Most of them live here at the clubhouse. They're kinda like friends with benefits for the members without old ladies. They're here for the guys who need a little attention."

"They what?"

"Not all the guys are into that sort of thing," Blair clarifies. "GP never touched the girls."

"And Eugene?"

Lindsey laughs. "I'm never going to get used to you calling him Eugene. I've called him Judge for as long as I could talk, and he's my blood relative." She takes a sip of her beer. "And yes, he's been with some. But he won't now that he's with you. My uncle is loyal."

My head spins as she rattles off more and more information, while I'm stuck inside my own head at the thought of any of these gorgeous women hanging all over Eugene in front of me. My heart sinks. He's been with the sweet butts, or whatever word she used to describe the scantily clad women who have popped in and out of the main room we've been sitting in. Is that what he would expect me to handle if we were together? To just be okay with other women trying to sleep with him right in front of me? Just the idea makes me want to walk right out the door and never look back. I may not be an expert in the relationship department, but I don't share.

I would have never thought that being with a biker could be so complicated.

Reaching out, Blair takes my hand and squeezes it. "It's confusing at first. It took me a while, but once you get used to it, it'll make more sense."

"It's like riding a bike," Lindsey assures me.

"It's more like trying to fly a plane with no experience, or pilots. Until you find the manual, you're kind of on your own to bring the nose up."

"You've been playing that flight simulator with the kids again, haven't you?"

"I don't mean to scare you away with all the club talk, but if you're going to be with him, you need to know. Being an old lady is one thing, but being the president's old lady is an entirely different animal. He leads the men. The president's old lady fills that role for the ladies. You'd be the first old lady if you're his."

My head spins. "I don't even know where I stand with him."

"No one ever does," Lindsey warns. "Club life isn't for everyone. Outsiders don't do well here."

"I was an outsider," Blair acknowledges.

"You're a different story."

"Ignore her, Grace. She's just protective of her uncle."

"Someone should be." Lindsey throws her hands up in the air. "He's had a lot of bad in his life. I want to make sure he doesn't get anymore."

I lean forward and catch Lindsey's eye, making sure she's listening to me when I speak. "Listen, I like Eugene a lot, actually, but I have no idea where this is going to go. We're still feeling it out... I think."

"Just don't hurt him. He seems to care for you. If you can't handle this, you need to tell him now before he gets in even deeper."

Is it really that obvious? We're attracted to each other, sure, but we barely know anything about each other. I don't even know his middle name or his birthday. How did we go from screwing around once to me leading the women of this club? If his own niece looks at me with such disdainful conviction, I assume others will too. He and I really need to talk.

"Enough about all that stuff," Blair asserts, her voice high and uncomfortable, and just the thing to break the tension in the air around us. "Tell us about you."

"There's really not much to tell, to be honest."

"Bullshit. My uncle wouldn't be that interested if you weren't something special."

"I really don't know why he's interested in me," I admit.

Blair takes a long look at me. "For one, you're stacked, and you've got this innocent librarian look going for you."

"I what?" I practically shriek, pulling my cardigan tight across my chest. Blair's bluntness is shocking. Do all women talk to each other like that? I've never really had close girlfriends to know if it is, or if it's just a biker chick thing. Whatever it is, I'm not sure I'm comfortable talking about my body like this.

"Can I ask you about your job?"

"What would you like to know?"

"How do you handle it? It has to be hard, ya know, being in the middle of the fray of broken families. While I deal with the aftermath in my line of work, you're there when the split happens."

"It's not easy. I used to be able to shut off my emotions and do my job, but I've realized recently that not every case calls for a removal."

"You mean Kevin and Natalie?"

"I do. A few days ago, if you would've told me I'd be here in this position, I'd have said you were off your rocker. But talking with Eugene and the kids, learning about everything they've been through from their own perspectives has changed mine."

"So why did you come here to remove them?"

"It was a court order. I'm bound by the law to do it, but I can't take them away from Eugene. Not after finding out the real truth of why they're with him."

"What will you do now?"

"Honestly, I don't know. The legal ways take too long, and the illegal ones are too dangerous. It's like a coin flip with no good options on either side. I'm not sure if your uncle told you, but I filed to be a foster parent. If my friend in the inspection office can get it pushed through, I can file to take legal custody of the kids while the issues with their father get worked out in court."

Lindsey's face falls. "My uncle wouldn't have custody if you did that. You could take them away any time you felt like it."

"I couldn't do that. Kevin and Natalie trust your uncle. They need him, yet he'd never get approved to be a foster parent with his record. But I can. It's the best option we have while the club deals with their father."

"You're risking your job, aren't you? Pushing through that application with your internal connections can't be legal."

I almost laugh. Nothing this club does errs on the side of legality, but here sits their president's own niece, questioning mine. Irony at its finest.

"I am, but if that's the price I have to pay, so be it.

They can't go with their father, and putting my trust in the legal system is too much of a chance. This is the only way." Even as the words slip past my lips, my candor shocks me. I know I've had my doubts about my job, but saying them out loud seems so foreign. I love my job, or I used to love it. But this case has given me an entirely new perspective on it all. Right now, Kevin and Natalie's safety is all that matters, with or without the law on my side.

"Well, if you're thinking about a career change, I could use someone with your dedication at the women's shelter I'm building. The non-profit paperwork was just approved last month, and I'm working on sourcing extra capital outside of what the club has agreed to pitch in to get me started," Blair mentions casually. "It's not much, but I hope to build on it in the future."

"I'll keep that in mind." Working without a paycheck would be hard, but it gives me an alternative to consider later. With so few things to spend my money on over the years, I have a decent nest egg. I could survive if something happened with my job, at least for a little while.

"I hope you do."

The door swings wide, and the three of us shift our focus to the men filing out in a line. Seeing me, Eugene makes his way over.

"The club's in, but I'm going to need you to stay with

me for a few days. I don't want you going anywhere alone."

"I don't need protection," I counter. "I'm a big girl."

His face doesn't waver at my joke. "I'm not taking no for an answer, Grace. I'll go get the kids, and we'll swing by your place to get your things. You'll be staying at my house."

He pivots away from me and heads for the hallway. I guess I understand why they call him Judge now.

## Judge

"BUT... we haven't seen our dad in years," Kevin says, his eyebrows squished together in confusion. "He took off when Nat was born. I don't even really remember him."

Natalie just stares ahead, her gaze unfocused.

Moving beside her, Grace wraps an arm around her shoulders. "Are you okay, honey?"

Natalie lays her head on Grace's shoulder. "I want to stay with Mr. Judge."

"You're not going anywhere, kiddo. You're staying with me. I won't let anyone take you away."

Natalie finally focuses her gaze, and when she does, she turns it on me. With a slow smile, she throws herself at me, wrapping her arms around my waist and hugging me tight. "You're our father, not him."

Her words hit me like a ton of bricks. But good

bricks. These kids haven't even been in my care for two months, and we're already a family. We argue sometimes. We laugh together. We play together. And most of all, we love each other.

"Damn right I am," I tell her, but my voice is thick with emotion.

"You kids go on up and get into bed. It's late."

"Goodnight, Grace. Goodnight, Mr. Judge," Natalie says with a musical lilt.

"Night," Kevin says, following his sister out of the room and down the hall.

Grace's eyes follow them before they disappear from view. "They're amazing kids. They've been through so much, but they're sweet, kind, and care about others."

"They're fucking incredible kids."

Grace smiles. "You're a pretty incredible father to them too."

Heat blooms in my chest. "*Fucking* incredible," I correct her.

She bites her lip, attempting to hide her smile. "Oh, excuse me. You're a *fucking* incredible father."

I lift my arm and flex my bicep. "Fucking right I am."

Grace's laughter fills the common area of the club-house, and a few of the guys look over. I can tell they don't trust her, seeing as she didn't exactly make a good first impression. But they will. Once they see the real

Grace—the one not hiding behind her glasses and a stack of case files—they'll realize she's a good woman.

"I never had a father," she tells me. "I was an orphan from the day I was born."

"What happened to your parents?"

"I'm not sure, really. And I think that's the worst part. There was no information in my file. Not their names, their ages. Nothing."

I take her hand in mine. "Is that normal?"

She gazes off into the distance, looking at nothing. "Nope."

"So you grew up in foster homes?"

"More than I care to count," she says sadly. "All over the state too. I never stayed in one place long enough to get settled."

"But they were good to you, right? I mean, not all foster homes are bad. And they're screened by DFPS."

"I had one good one, Mrs. Rosenburg. She was a retired school teacher. Her husband had passed away a couple of years before she'd taken me in. She was really nice. An excellent cook too."

Though she's right beside me, her voice may as well be a thousand miles away. "You don't have to talk about this, darlin'."

"No." Pulling herself out of her thoughts, she meets my gaze. "Sorry. When I talk about that, I get so lost in the memories. Mrs. Rosenburg always had a batch of freshly baked cookies on the counter when I got home from school each day. But whenever I try to remember the good things, it's always squashed by one other memory. I guess this time is no different."

Digging her fingers into her knees, she takes a deep breath and blows it out slowly. "She had a heart attack while I was at school. I found her on the kitchen floor. The cookies were burning in the oven, and it was too late to save her."

"Jesus."

"It devastated me when I found her. I didn't even care when they sent me off to another place—a group home that time."

"You've had it rough."

"I have, but others have had it far, far worse. I was lucky enough to come out okay in the end."

I give her shoulder a playful shove. "Says you."

Sticking out her tongue at me, she huffs, "Bite me, biker. Now it's your turn. What's your story?"

I groan. I hadn't expected to spill my guts tonight. "I'm not that interesting."

"Baloney. Tell me how Eugene Grant came to be such an incredible man and father figure." She waves her hand around, indicating the rest of the common room. "Not just to those kids, either. These men look to you like a father too."

I rarely share the details of my past. In fact, I've spoken my truth a grand total of two times in my life. This will be the third.

"It's not pretty," I warn her.

"Yeah, and mine was all sunshine and rainbows," she quips. Her words are sarcastic, but she moves to place her hand in mine, somehow able to tell this is going to be hard on me.

"I married my high school sweetheart." Her eyes widen. "It was no great love or anything. To be honest, I don't even know why we got married in the first place. We cared about each other, spent a lot of time together. When we graduated high school, I was prospecting with the club, and she wanted to tie me to her forever."

I note her disapproving frown, but I don't stop. I need to get this out.

"It was stupid. We fought all the time. We had no money, and she was always off drinking with friends and getting her hair done." Now the hard part. "And then she had Shane."

Her body jolts, her mouth opening to speak, but I raise my hand to stop her.

"Just let me get this out," I tell her. "Shane was the sweetest baby. When he came along, I vowed to work harder to save my marriage. I was going to be the best father in the entire world."

"What happened?"

"He died." Looking down, I examine my fingernails, not really seeing them. "I was just a prospect back then and was out on a run. When I came home..." I pause, trying to swallow the lump in my throat. The pain is as great today as it was nearly thirty years ago. "She'd already buried him, said she didn't know how to get a hold of me."

Gaping at me, she covers her mouth and whispers, "How did he pass away?"

I shrug. "SIDS. She never gave me an explanation other than that. I tried to find out where he was buried, but every time I asked, she would scream and rant at me about leaving them alone in the first place. She left a month later, and the last I heard, she'd died of an overdose, which wasn't too long ago."

Her mouth opens and closes, and she finally says, "Wow," seeming at a loss for words.

"Yeah. Wow."

We're both silent for a few moments, which is strange in itself since everyone else in the room is drinking and laughing, and having a great time. But it's like we're alone here. In a bubble. A bubble of confessions, sadness, and acceptance.

Acceptance is a new one for me. I don't think I've ever experienced acceptance.

Rubbing my hand, she says with sincerity, "I'm sorry about your son, Eugene."

I blow out a shaky breath. "I'm sorry about your parents."

Her lips graze mine for a fraction of a second. "Thank you for telling me about Shane."

Hearing his name said out loud is like a tiny stitch in the gaping wound left from his passing. That wound has never healed, and I've never spoken about it. Maybe that's why it still hurts, like it just happened yesterday.

Leaning over, I press my lips against her forehead, thankful for her and the way things have worked out.

When I'd first met Grace, I thought she would be my biggest nightmare, but it's starting to look like she may just be my salvation instead.

Grace

BUZZ. Buzz. Buzz.

That's all my phone has been doing since I called off work again. If it's not Eric, it's Aaron, one right after another. It's like the two of them are in constant communication about my whereabouts now. Eric, I can understand, as I never call off work. Ever. I've worked with my head in a trash can after getting food poisoning before, so calling off multiple days in a row is out of the ordinary for me. I know I'll have to come up with some plausible reason for being out so many days soon, or he'll send out for a wellness check on me.

Aaron calls again, and I send him straight to voicemail. The fourteenth voicemail notification this morning pops up on the screen. I swipe it away to ignore it. *Take the hint, buddy. I'm busy.*

Setting my phone down on the table, I watch as Eugene works with Kevin on some math problems his school sent over at the kitchen table. How he convinced them that the kids were very ill and would likely be out for a few weeks, I'll never know. But whatever he did, the teachers sent homework every day to their school email accounts.

Catching me watching them, he pats his big hand on top of the table and winks back at me. My face flushes instantly at his reminder of what we did on that very table just a few nights ago. Seeing this, his smile only gets bigger.

I roll my eyes at his distance flirting and return to helping Natalie with her reading. She sits calmly next to me, reading aloud from a chapter book she had brought home from school. She sounds out each word carefully, but stops every few sentences to ask me for help. She has a lot of catching up to do. Thanks to her uncle, she's academically stunted, and it isn't going to be easy to get her where she should be. Until things get settled, though, Eugene and I are doing what we can to help them both.

The crunch of a vehicle pulling up to the front of the house draws my attention. Pushing aside the sheer curtain behind me, I watch as a black sedan with dark windows park directly behind Eugene's motorcycle.

"Eugene," I call out. "Someone's here."

Pushing away from the table, he takes long strides into the living room. Not quite running, but definitely in a hurry. He peers through the curtain.

"Kevin," he snaps. "Take your sister and do what I told you to do when we talked."

My heart sinks to my feet. "What's going on?"

"Police," he bites out. "Kevin. Move, son."

Running into the room, he grabs Natalie by the arm and tugs. "Come on. You need to come with me."

"I don't want to leave," she cries, shoving Kevin away. "I want to stay with you."

Eugene sighs. "Nat, go. Now. And stay with Kevin. I'll come get you when it's safe." Setting her book down on the table, she follows her brother to the back of the house.

My heart thumps in my ears as I hear heavy footsteps trudging up the front sidewalk, and then a loud pounding rattles the door. Eugene's hand slips to the back of his jeans, resting on a handgun tucked into the back of them. Shifting off of the couch, I stand behind him.

"Open up! I know she's in there," Aaron's voice booms from the other side of the door.

*Oh my God.* If I could crawl into a gaping hole in the ground, I would. An angry heat sets me on fire from the inside out as I step around Eugene and put myself between him and the door. Between him, his gun, and Aaron.

My hand trembles as I reach for the knob. Eugene's hand comes down hard on top of mine, stopping me.

"I can hear you on the other side of the door, mother-fucker. I swear to God, if you're holding her there, I'll personally haul your ass to jail. Open up!" He pounds so hard, the photo hanging on the wall near the door crashes to the floor, sending shattered glass around my feet.

"He won't leave if I don't talk to him," I whisper. "Please, let me take care of this."

The stubborn man doesn't budge, a tiny vein in his forehead visibly throbbing.

"Please, Eugene," I beg him. "He won't go away until he sees me. Stay inside, I beg you."

I brush away his hand, and this time, he allows it. When he steps back, I turn the knob and pull the door open. Aaron's dark eyes are filled with fiery anger, but flash with relief when he sees me. Stepping out, I quickly yank the door behind me closed, leaving Eugene safely inside.

"What are you doing here?"

"I could ask you the same thing."

I try to keep my cool. If Aaron knew what lies on the other side of the door, he'll bust in there after him and take the kids out of spite. I have to talk him down. Taking a gigantic step toward me, I back up against the door. I can almost feel the heat radiating off of Eugene from the other side as Aaron's gaze trails up and down my body, looking for some sign that I'm being held against my will.

"How did you find me?"

Grabbing his phone out of his pocket, he waves it in front of me. I look at, confused. Hashtag had turned off my GPS, so that shouldn't be possible.

"I pinged your phone, and after I searched your apartment, I found this address written on a pad of paper."

"Wait a second. You broke into my apartment?" I bellow. "How dare you!"

"Wellness check," he snaps. "Your super let me in. I wouldn't have had to do that if you'd answered your fucking phone."

A coil of anger unfurls inside of me. It wasn't a wellness check. He intruded into my private space and abused his power to do it. The nerve of him.

"So what?" I snarl, throwing my arms wide. "You're stalking me now? I'm allowed to have a life, Aaron. One where I do *not* need to inform you of my every move. You're crossing a line right now. You need to leave."

"I know whose house this is, Grace. It doesn't take a rocket scientist to figure it out. Why don't you step aside and let me take care of him so you can go back to your life?"

He tries to sidestep me, but I stay put. He's not going into that house. I won't allow it.

"What exactly do you think you know about my life?"

His eyes narrow. "Enough to know that this case is clouding your judgment, and that you need a healthy dose of reality to help you realize you're in danger."

Oh, this ought to be good. "Explain to me, how I'm in danger?"

He tips his head at the door. "That man will get you killed, Grace."

"He's protected me more than you ever could have."

"How? He's the bad guy in this, not me."

"You couldn't be more wrong. That man has protected me and those kids."

Aaron's face stills. "That's twice you've said that. How has he protected you?"

Folding my arms across my chest, I let him have it. "Their father tried to take me hostage a few days ago at the coffee shop next to the office. Eugene scared him off. If he hadn't, there's no telling what that man would've done to me. He's a junkie, and he's dangerous. I probably wouldn't be standing here right now yelling at you if it weren't for Eugene."

"Oh, come on. That doesn't change who he is or what he's capable of."

"Let me tell you who Eugene Grant really is. He's a hard-ass of a man who loves those kids more than anyone on this planet could. If it weren't for him, Natalie would've been sold into a sex trafficking ring. Kevin would have turned out just like their uncle who forced them both into it. If he and his club hadn't stepped in, neither one of those kids would be in one piece right now. He saved them. He's protected them. If that's not the definition of what a father should be, then I've failed as a social worker."

He takes a step back. "You knew all this, and you didn't bring it to me? I could have fucking helped you, Grace."

"No, you couldn't have. Only the Black Hoods could help me."

Aaron blinks once, twice. "What exactly can they give you that I can't?"

"Safety," I reply. "The ability to do what I need to do to protect these kids."

"You're breaking the law."

I laugh, without an ounce of humor. "The law is already broken. It has been for a really long time." Everything I've held back from him the last few years continues to flow out of me like a raging river after a heavy spring storm. "I've watched family after family being torn apart. For once, I want to keep this one together. They can protect them."

Aaron's nostrils flare. "They're not his to protect." Spittle flies from his mouth as he raises his voice. I've never heard him yell before, but somehow, I'm not surprised he has such a short fuse. "And neither are you."

"That's for me to decide, not you."

What happens next, happens so fast, I don't have time to register it.

Aaron's fist rockets toward me, dangerously close to my face, but only the breeze from its power caresses my cheek before landing against the door behind me.

His eyes fall closed when he realizes what he's done. "Grace, I'm sorry. I didn't mean to do that."

I feel the support of the door fall away and land against Eugene's body, shaking with rage. "I will fucking rip your head off and shit down your neck," he growls.

Aaron's eyes grow wide.

"No!" I cry, turning to face Eugene. Placing my hands on his chest, I stare deep into his eyes, searching through the fiery anger for some form of reasoning. "Don't. I'm okay."

Eugene's skin is burning beneath my palms, and for a

fraction of a second, I fear he won't listen to me. Finally, he looks at me, inspecting me for himself, his hand moving possessively over my skin in front of Aaron. He's staking his claim without having to say the words. "I'm okay," I promise. "He didn't hit me. He hit the door."

"Real fucking men don't even do that," he growls. "Do you hear me, asshole? What you just did is the next worst fucking thing to hitting a woman. Scaring her and making her think you're going to is a coward's move."

Aaron doesn't reply. I turn to face him, but Eugene's arms wrap tight around my waist.

"You need to leave."

His voice is deflated now. Weak. "Grace, I came here for you."

"And you're leaving without her," Eugene snarls from behind me. Aaron takes a step back, but hesitates to move any farther.

"Why him? Why couldn't I be that man for you? I tried to be, but you never let me in. I fucking love you, Grace."

"I don't love you, and I never will. You just didn't want to accept that. No matter how hard you push I'm never going to feel that way about you."

"But you can love him? A criminal."

"I care about him, yes, and his past doesn't matter to me. Only the future and these kids matter now."

His eyes glass over with sadness as he looks between us. "Take care of her." Turning, he walks away from us and back to his car. Lingering just inside his open car door, he slides in behind the wheel and drives away, and out of my life.

Chapter 26

Judge

HER FINGERS DIG into my hair as her hips roll. "God, please, don't stop."

Oh, there's no way in hell I'm stopping.

Dragging my tongue between her folds, I press a soft kiss to the sensitive pearl nestled deep within, making her moan. Fuck me, she's incredible.

Using my lips, I pull her clit this way and that, flicking it gently with my tongue, reveling in her taste. I could live right here, between her legs, feasting on the buffet that's her perfect fucking body.

Her thighs tremble and her moans get louder, and finally, I can't take it anymore.

Standing at the end of the bed, I pull her to me, raising her feet high in the air, and enter her hard. She's so fucking tight. I thrust faster, loving the way her breasts bounce, her nipples tight and swollen from my earlier kisses.

Grace's eyes are locked on mine, her face twisted with a pleasure that mirrors my own.

"Fuck," I bite out, not sure how much more I can take. I've always considered myself to have pretty great stamina, but with Grace... fuck, the woman undoes me. Sex with her makes me feel like a sixteen-year-old boy, for fuck's sake.

A deafening crash, followed by the sound of shattered glass hitting the ceramic tile, rips us from our moment. Our heads whip toward the bedroom door in shock.

"What was that?" Grace whispers, her eyes wide with fear. I'm already on the move.

Yanking my jeans on, I move to the door with my gun in hand before Grace even has a chance to pull my T-shirt over her head.

"Stay here," I tell her, but I'm already focused on the sounds that aren't yet coming from the front hall.

And then I hear it. A heavy boot crunching down on the broken glass as somebody enters my house.

Bad move, pal.

"Eugene!" she whisper-cries as I slip out of the bedroom and down the hall, my gun up and ready to fire.

My mind races as I listen. Who could this be? Is this the same person who broke the window out at the garage?

Is it that fucker, Aaron? Whoever it is, he's bold. He's pulling this shit in broad daylight, and could've been seen by any number of nosy neighbors on this block.

Slow, careful footsteps creep toward the hallway, and I wait. I don't want to give the son of a bitch a chance to run out the front door.

When a shadow crosses the floor close to me, I make my move.

Jumping out from the hall, I aim my gun, my feet planted apart, ready to fire.

But Henry Tucker couldn't care less. He doesn't stop. He storms toward me, a gun clenched in his own hand, his face twisted with derangement and pure anger.

Before I know what's hit me, my gun is flying to the ground somewhere out of reach and Henry's on top of me, biting, scratching, and clawing at me. The sounds coming from his throat are terrifying. I've never heard noises like that come from a human being.

His hands go around my throat, and we both fall to the ground in a struggle. There isn't a lot of room in my tiny living room, and every which way I roll, wanting to take this asshole by surprise and get him off of me, ends with us slamming into a wall or a large piece of furniture. I'm trapped beneath him.

Henry's eyes are red and empty of everything, except his rage. When he pulls his fist back, getting ready to slam it down into my face, I realize how much danger we're both in.

Grace is somewhere close by.

Henry Tucker's fist bashes into my skull once, twice, and then a third time. The ringing in my ears grows, but still, I fight.

I've been in my share of fistfights, and I've never lost one. I'm not about to lose this one, either.

"Eugene!" Grace shrieks.

Henry's head whips up to look at her, and I take my shot. I fist his hair in my hand, twisting it in my fingers as close to the scalp as I can manage and throw him off balance.

Using the momentum, I push with my legs to toss him up and over me. I jump to my feet, rushing to get my gun, but Henry reaches his first.

"Don't you fucking move!" he screams. Looking back, I find him standing with his gun aimed directly at Grace. My heart sinks as I freeze. I couldn't move now if I wanted to.

"Get over there and stand with her," he orders, waving the gun between us. "Now!"

As I approach Grace, I stare into her pale, terrified face, wondering how I could have fucked this up so bad. I fucked up, and now she's in danger. We may not make it out of here alive.

## Chapter 27

Grace

"YOU DON'T HAVE to do this," I plead, pressing my back against the wall, my fingers like claws in the back of Eugene's shirt.

Henry's lips move, spouting off unintelligible words, but he doesn't lower the gun. "Where are my fucking kids, bitch?"

Eugene lifts a hand, turning the psycho's attention onto himself. "Calm down, buddy. Let's work this out like adults. Nobody has to get hurt here."

Henry's lips stop moving as he lowers the gun to his side, but his whole body trembles with aggression. "My kids. They're my kids, not yours. Mine. Give them to me."

I tug on Eugene's shirt, pulling him tight against me.

With the blood pounding in my ears, the room around me spins as I force myself to stay still and calm.

"Gene, look what Karma got me!"

Kevin pushes through the back door and into the kitchen before I can stop him, with Natalie right behind him. The moment she lays eyes on Henry, she screeches to a halt. My heart plummets.

Things just went from bad to a million times worse.

"This kid's gonna be a—" Karma stops mid-sentence and quickly pushes Lindsey behind him.

Oh God. Now we're all here. Six of us held hostage by a man who's obviously tweaking and has a loaded gun.

"Well, who do we have here?" Henry smiles when he notices Lindsey. I watch in horror as every drop of blood drains from Lindsey's face when Henry reaches for her.

"Leave her alone," Karma growls. "She's pregnant."

Karma moves to intercept Henry, and that's when the loudest sound I've ever heard blasts through the room, leaving my ears ringing.

For a moment, I don't understand what's happened or where that sound had come from, but as a red circle blossoms and grows on the front of Karma's T-shirt, I know. My screams mix with those of Lindsey's and the kids' as Karma gapes at Eugene. Dropping to his knees, he falls forward, landing directly on his face.

"Nobody move!" Henry roars, now pointing the gun at Lindsey as he yanks at his hair with his free hand, moaning as if in agony. "Oh fuck, fuck, fuck. Oh, God."

I stare at Karma's motionless body, and send a silent prayer out into the universe, begging for him to be okay. Everyone's sobbing except for Eugene, who looks ready to throw himself into battle, gun or no gun.

"You killed him," Lindsey cries. "You fucking killed him, you son of a bitch!" Tears stream down her face, but she looks heartbroken. She leans forward, as if to check on Karma, but then she's on the ground before the sound of another gunshot even registers in my mind.

"No!" I scream. "Please, stop!"

Lindsey wails, clutching her stomach, and Karma's words from just a few seconds ago repeat over and over in my mind. *She's pregnant. She's pregnant. Lindsey's pregnant.*

*No, no, no!* This can't be happening.

Kevin and Natalie stare down at her, their faces frozen in shock, their eyes glistening with tears.

"Kevin?" Henry asks, his voice going from psychopath to sweet as sugar. "Natalie? Remember me? I'm your father."

Kevin looks back down at Lindsey and Karma, both of them lying in their own puddles of blood getting bigger by the second.

"Natalie?" he asks again, this time reaching out and stroking her hair. "Baby, I'm your daddy." Natalie sobs and shrinks away from his touch.

Whatever hold Eugene had been keeping on his temper disappears in that instant. A growl of rage ripping from his throat, he moves toward Henry once again, but Henry is fast. Inhumanly fast.

I've seen it before when someone's high on meth or something similar. They become extremely fast and incredibly strong. But I've never seen anyone move as fast as Henry.

"Henry, no!" I scream as he brings the butt of his gun down on Eugene's skull. Grabbing onto the children, I shove them behind me, unable to believe what I'm seeing.

My mind races for a way out of this at the same time my heart stutters in my chest as Eugene crumbles like an accordion and falls into a heap onto the floor.

"Oh my God, Eugene," I sob. "Please, say something." I watch helplessly as a single drop of blood falls from his temple and onto the hardwood floor.

I want to go to him. I want to make sure he's okay, but I can't. I can't because I'm the only thing standing in the way of Henry Tucker and his kids. I have to keep my shit together before I end up like the others. All I can do is watch and pray. Pray for all of us. Pray that I can find a way out of this.

My body trembles uncontrollably while I stare at his chest, desperate to be sure he's still breathing. Seconds feel like years until his chest heaves once. Twice. It's labored, but he's alive. Eugene is still with me.

Henry turns away from him with a sick, satisfied smile.

"It's just me and you now, Grace," he slurs, stepping closer to me. "You and me. You and me," he mutters to himself. "This didn't have to happen, you know. All you had to do was give me my kids. *My* kids. Not yours. Not his." He points his handgun in Eugene's direction. "All I want is my kids!" Rubbing the gun against the side of his face, Eugene's blood drips from the butt of it and onto his skin. Wiping it away with his other hand, he looks down with a sickening smile.

He steps toward me, and Natalie presses tighter against my backside, while Kevin tries to push in front of me, but I shove him back. He's been a hero for his sister long enough. He needs a hero to take care of him too. This is my fight now.

Setting his eyes on Natalie, Henry reaches out his hand, beckoning her. "You're a pretty little thing, aren't you? A looker like your mama."

"Leave her alone," Kevin snarls.

Henry's lips pull back, baring his rotting teeth. "You shut your fucking mouth!"

He charges toward us, and I shift in response, moving us closer to the open kitchen entry. If I could just get us a little closer, I can distract him and get the kids out that way. It's the only shot we have with him blocking the front door.

I thrust out my hands in front of us. "Take me," I beg him.

Screeching to a halt, he tilts his head to the side. "What the hell am I going to do with an old bitch like you? My buyers want young, pretty little things like her."

I gape at him. "You don't mean... You're her father!"

Sell her. *Oh my God.* He doesn't want them back to take care of them. He's a trafficker, just like their uncle.

His words from our first conversation pops into my head. *I lost my business when she left.* That's what he meant. She took his cash cow when she took the kids. He's been planning to sell Natalie since the day she was born.

"Why the fuck do you think I want her? I never wanted kids in the first place. That bitch started pumping them out like a fucking vending machine. Randall fucked me over big time when he didn't make his sale at the border, and now they're coming after me to collect. She's my only fucking option."

"You can't have her!" Kevin screams. "I won't let you do it!"

"Who's going to stop me, boy? You? Her?" He presses the gun into my chest. "I'm going to kill your friend Grace, and then I'll sell you to someone who likes pretty little boys."

"Henry, listen to me. These are your children. This is just the drugs talking."

He digs the barrel of the gun in deeper. "Shut the fuck up! You're just like their whore mother, always trying to tell me what to fucking do."

"I'm sorry. I know what she did was wrong. She should have never taken the kids away from you," I lie, but the words still burn like acid on my tongue.

"She deserved what she got. I'd have done it if Randall hadn't beaten me to it."

That's how their uncle got them. He killed their mom to get them, just like their father has done here. There's no way out of this. Death means nothing to this man. The only way these kids will make it out of here alive is if I do something drastic. The plan forms in my mind. The kitchen has a back exit, and we're only a few feet away from the entrance. If I could only get us closer, I could charge him, and the kids could escape out the back. I have to keep him talking, keep him focused on me while I enact my plan.

"I know she did. She was a horrible person." With each word, I take a small step back, inching us closer to the doorway. Kevin tugs hard on my shirt, but I can't answer him. I can't acknowledge him. The second Henry's focus slips from me, it's all over for us. So I do the only thing that I can. I ignore it.

"He should've let me kill her!" he bellows, dropping to his knees and clutching his head between his hands, screaming into the floorboards. With his focus turned away from us, I take two big steps, herding the kids behind me until both slip into the opening of the kitchen.

Reaching back, I grab Kevin's hand, giving it a hard squeeze before I scream, "Run!"

The next few seconds are a blur. Kevin and Natalie slip out of the room as I charge Henry. His eyes raise from the floor just before I tackle him.

He shoves at me, trying to get to his feet, but I keep fighting. I claw at him, bite him, doing anything I can to keep him down long enough for the kids to get away. The gun slips from his grasp with a *clank* next to my head, and I scramble for it on my hands and knees.

Just as I'm about to close my hands around the butt, Henry's on me. His foot slams into my chest, kicking me back as he reaches for the gun.

I gasp for air, but I know that if he gets that gun before I do, it's over. With as much strength as I can muster, I reach for him again, but he moves so fast. The gun is at my temple before I can get to my feet, and the hammer clicks back.

"You stupid bitch," he spits, his finger dancing on the trigger in slow motion. I close my eyes, waiting for the world to disappear around me, finding peace because my sacrifice won't be in vain. The kids got away. They'll live on.

A heavy *thunk* echoes through the room, followed by the thud of Henry's body hitting the ground beside me. I whip around in shock to find Kevin shaking like a leaf, a cast iron pan clutched in his hands.

"Holy shit," he whispers.

Sirens wail in the distance as I stare at the carnage around us.

## Judge

"JUST STITCH IT UP. I'll be fine."

The doctor rolls his eyes. "Sir, I get it, you're tough, but you have a severe concussion, three fractured ribs, and a deep laceration on your scalp."

I glare at him. "So stitch the laceration, and I'll be careful with the rest. My family is out there with worse injuries than mine, and I need to be there for them."

"I'll take care of him," Grace assures the frustrated doctor.

Nodding, he sets out to stitch the wound left on my forehead by the butt of Henry's gun.

"Lindsey?" I ask, turning my attention to Grace.

Her mouth turns down. "She was pregnant." It's no less of a shock now as it was when Karma had said it to Henry Tucker earlier.

"You said *was*. Is the baby okay?"

A tear falls from her eye and down her cheek. "She lost the baby."

"Is Lindsey going to live?" I ask her, my teeth clenched as the doctor starts in with the sutures.

"Sir," he admonishes. "If you don't stay still, you're going to be in here even longer when I accidentally punch this needle through your eye. Stop moving!"

Grace and I both ignore him. "Yes, Eugene, Lindsey is going to survive, but the bullet destroyed her womb. She not only lost her baby, but she'll never be able to have another one. She's devastated."

Devastated, I can deal with. At least she's alive to be devastated.

"And Karma?"

"We don't know yet. He's in surgery."

"Is he going to make it?" I demand.

Another tear slides down her cheek. "We just don't know. If you're the praying kind, though, this is the time to do it."

I gape at her in shock. Karma is one of my best buddies. He's a good shit. Reliable. Funny. Always ready to help out with a slap for Twat Knot when he's being an ass. I don't think I can handle life without him in it.

"Kevin and Natalie are out in the hall," she continues,

dashing away her tears and forcing a shaky smile onto her lips. "They were so brave, Eugene. You should be proud of them. And Kevin..." She takes a deep breath and blows it out slowly. "Kevin saved my life. He saved all of us."

"You almost done, Doc?" I feel like I'm about to crawl out of my bruised and battered skin. I just want to see my kids, reassure myself that they're really okay. I want to go to Lindsey and hold her, tell her everything is going to be okay. I want to get the hell out of here so I can be there when Karma comes out of surgery.

"Yeah, yeah, Rambo, keep your chaps on."

Grace stares at me with wide eyes, stifling a laugh behind her hand. Gazing up at the doc, I raise my brow. "You're a brave man, Doc."

He shakes his head. "Nah. I'm just tired of people bitching at me to move faster when I'm doing my damn job."

I'm in no mood for his annoyance, so I open my mouth to tell him exactly what I think about him and his damn job, but Grace beats me to it.

"He's sorry, Doctor. We've just had a very rough night, and some of the others that were with us are hurt badly."

Grabbing a pair of odd-looking scissors, he brings them to my head, cuts the thread, and winds some gauze around my noggin over and over again. "There. All done."

I hop down off the table and follow Grace to the door.

"If you feel nauseous at all, you get your butt back in here," the doctor calls out as we round the corner.

Kevin and Natalie are right outside, just as Grace had said. I don't know which one of them hugs me tighter, but I don't even care. My arms wrap around those kids and I hold them against my fractured chest, ignoring the pain and just reveling in the fact that my kids are here, and that I still have them with me.

"I was so scared," Natalie sobs into my blood-stained shirt.

"Me too, kiddo. Me too."

She looks up at me, surprised. "You were scared?"

"Terrified. I thought he was going to hurt us and take you guys away. I thought he was going to hurt you both."

Kevin's eyes flash with anger. "He hurt Karma and Lindsey."

Swallowing hard, I follow Grace as she leads us all down a long corridor. "I know, but that's all he was able to do." I reach over and place my hand on Kevin's shoulder as we walk. "You did good, bud. So fucking good."

"I didn't save Karma and Lindsey, or their baby," he mumbles.

Their *baby? Lindsey's baby was Karma's?* I knew he had a thing for her, but he'd never once come to me and told me he was going to pursue it. Probably because he knew I'd rip his fucking dick off.

"You were amazing," Grace assures him.

We enter the waiting area on the third floor of the hospital a few moments later, where leather clad bikers are sprawled out around the room. Some are asleep, and some are awake, mumbling to each other, all of them looking worried.

"Have we heard anything?" Their heads whip up, and one by one they come to me, slapping me on the back. It sounds nice in theory, but with broken ribs, they might as well be stabbing me right in the chest.

"Glad you're okay, man," GP says, going in for the final hug of the group. "You just missed the doc about twenty minutes ago. He said Karma is out of surgery, but for now, it's touch and go. He took a bullet directly to the heart."

Natalie sobs beside me, and Grace wraps her arm around her shoulders, pulling her into her side.

"They got the bullet and stopped the bleeding. They fixed it as best they could." GP sighs. "He's in a medically induced coma, and will be for the next few days. His heart needs time to heal, and he'd be in too much pain if they let him wake up now."

"Is he going to live?" Grace asks.

"It's too early to tell."

I look over at Stone Face, whose anger always seems to simmer just under the surface. "What happened to Henry Tucker?"

"Cops arrested him before we even got there," he bites out. "He's locked up at the station tonight, but will probably be off to county before lunchtime tomorrow."

I narrow my eyes and step closer so only he can hear me. "We can't let this slide."

"Oh, we aren't. Trust me. But once he hits county, it's going to take some effort to get to him. It won't be easy."

"Mr. Grant?" a nurse calls from the locked door leading down to the patient rooms. "Your niece would like to see you."

I make my way toward her, squeezing Grace's hand as I go. I don't know what to think about Lindsey and this whole baby thing. I mean, she's a grown ass woman. She can make her own choices. She taught me that back when she was just a teenager. If I had to describe Lindsey in one word, it would be independent. But if it was Karma's baby that she lost? That's a whole different story.

I follow the nurse down the hall and around the corner. Finally, we stop outside of the room. "She's very emotional," the nurse warns, and then, without even giving me a chance to absorb that unwelcome information, she shoves the door open and steps inside.

Lindsey's curled on her side, a pillow clutched to her chest. She's not crying, but it doesn't take a rocket scientist to see she's been doing a lot of it recently.

Her head lifts when she sees me, and she starts to cry. "You're okay?"

Moving to her side, I wrap her in my arms. "I'm okay, darlin'. Are you okay?"

Her voice breaks as she tells me, "I lost my baby."

I don't know what to say, so I say nothing other than, "I know, sweetheart. I know." Holding her tight, I ignore the pain I feel from my own wounds and rock her gently from side to side.

"Nothing's ever going to be the same again, is it?"

And that's when I realize that no, it won't be. The cops have arrested Henry. Karma's in a coma. Lindsey will never have children, which is something she's always wanted. And my kids will never have peace until they know he's gone. Not in jail, but gone.

As a father, I need to make sure my kids get their peace, no matter what.

## Grace

I NEVER THOUGHT this day would come. The day I would walk into my office for the last time. While a part of me has pangs of sadness for all the years of work I've lost to this place, the future in front of me lessens it.

I scan the four walls that are filled with memories. Good, bad, and in-between.

I've done good things here.

I've seen the worst.

I survived.

I pull out one of my desk drawers and double check that all of its contents are securely nestled in the box on my desk. A noise draws my attention to the door. Eric leans against it with a frown on his face.

"Grace," he mumbles before shoving his way inside.

"Eric."

"I thought I'd come see you off."

"That's nice of you," I lie. He's only here because it's mandated for anyone who puts in their notice.

"Are you sure this is what you want?" I hear it in his voice that he wants me to reconsider.

"It is," I declare. I broke the rules. All the rules, actually. And to be honest, it felt good that I helped bring a family together instead of tearing it apart with a lot of help from Eugene and his club. "It's time, Eric. I'm ready for a change." More like, there's no way in hell they'd allow me to stay employed here when they figured out whose bed I'm sharing. It's not like I can hide the big beast of a man from this side of my life. They could call my judgment into question as a key witness for future cases because of my association with the club. No. This is the best thing for all of us.

"What will you do now?"

"I have a job offer. A good one."

"Oh, wow. That was fast. Any place I know?"

"Nope." Grabbing a photo on the edge of my desk made by one of the kids I'd helped reunite with her dad, I stuff it into the almost overflowing box. "It's the change of pace I need. After so many years, it's going to be nice to help people again."

Eric arches an eyebrow in confusion. "We help people every day."

"Eric, be honest. When's the last time you felt good about our line of work? When you really felt like you helped protect the happiness of the kids who come into our care? Don't you get tired of watching families being torn apart over some technicality?"

"We are helping them, Grace. We protect them from abuse. Homelessness. Poor living conditions. Happiness isn't a factor in what we do." Taking a deep breath, he shrugs. It's like he's reading the recruiting handbook back to me verbatim. The old Grace would've believed every single word of his spiel. I know better than that now.

"I thought being in their shoes would help provide a deeper perspective into what they're going through, but do you know what I realized? The system hasn't changed. A lying parent can rip away the rights of the other parent whenever they want. We send a child into foster care when their grandmother wants to care for them. How are we protecting them?"

"We're bound by the law, you know that."

"Well, I'm tired of laws that only work for those who know how to manipulate them to fit their own agenda."

"Jesus, Grace. Is that how you see it?"

"You really are blind to it all now. It's a shame. You used to be such a good advocate for these kids, but the life of bureaucracy gets us all, I guess."

"Where is this coming from? This isn't the Grace Halfpenny I know. What's changed?"

What hasn't changed about me? I'm happy. I have a family. It may be a little non-traditional, but it's a family. One that looks out for each other in their own ways. It's not the kind of family I was looking for, but it's the one I've needed all along.

"Family. I have a family for the first time in my life." He stares at me again with confusion. "That's where I've been, Eric. I wasn't sick. I was protecting my family, and do you know what I learned? That the last few weeks have been more fulfilling to me than the last ten years I've spent here."

Shoving the last stack of my personal files into the box, I place the lid on top and pick it up.

"If you'll excuse me, I have to pick the kids up from school. My keys, badge, and anything else you need are in the top drawer of the desk. Have a nice life, Eric."

I hurry toward the door and shove my way past him without even saying goodbye or looking at him. I stare straight ahead, all the way out of the office and to my car. My mind is elsewhere, and I don't even notice the man leaning against my car.

"Where the hell have you been?" Greg's voice cuts into the haze. I jump out of my skin, nearly dropping the box.

"Jesus, Greg! Where did you come from?" I exclaim, trying to keep the box from tumbling onto the ground. "You scared the crap out of me."

"I could ask you the same thing." Pushing away from my car, he takes the box from my hands and sets it down on the ground next to my feet. "You been dodging me?"

"I'm sorry. I've been busy the last couple of weeks, Greg. Things have been a bit complicated with work."

"I didn't know 'work' rode a motorcycle. Shit must be different at the office since the last time I stopped by."

"How did you know?"

He scowls, his weathered face looking serious. "Someone has to look out for you. I saw him bring you to the office. He treat you okay? Because if he doesn't, I can still kick an ass or two at my age."

I try not to laugh at the thought of Greg squaring off against Eugene. It'll only upset his cranky ass even more if he thinks I'm laughing at him and not at the idea of it.

"He does, and he's done so much for me."

"You love him, don't you?"

"I do," I admit. "He's rough around the edges, but he sees me for me. He understands me, as crazy as that sounds."

"That's good, Grace. But the offer still stands. He hurts you, I'll show him what they taught me in Nam."

"I'll let him know. How about I bring him with me next week? I'll bring enough burgers for all of us."

"I won't be there."

"What do you mean?" What's changed in the last couple of weeks that Greg isn't going to be in his normal haunt? I check him over, and nothing has visibly changed.

"I'm going to the VA."

"You're what? Oh, Greg, that's great. What made you change your mind?"

"You're taken care of now." How did that stop him from going to the VA? I've been after him for years, and that's why?

"You refused to go because of me?" How in the world would I be the reason behind that? "I don't understand."

"I had a daughter once. Elizabeth. Bitty, as I liked to call her. When I came home from the war, she and her mother were both gone. I tried to find them, but I never did. I went to war, and she left me without so much as a goodbye."

"I'm so sorry," I nearly sob. "I had no idea." He never really talked about himself or his family. How much more do I not know about him?

"You remind me of her." My heart shatters inside my chest. He's been through so much, and I never even scratched the surface of how bad it's been for him. I knew he was alone, but not like this. Not in this way. "You even smile like her."

"If you ever want to find her again, I might be able to help. There's so many different ways to track someone down now."

"I'll consider it."

As he walks away, I call out, "You never answered my question, Greg. Why am I the reason you didn't go to the VA?"

"Someone had to watch out for you, and now that you've found yourself a man, I can finally retire from the post."

"I don't know what to say. I didn't know that's why you didn't want to go."

"Don't go making a fuss about it," he scoffs. "You gotta make me a promise, though. You'll still come to visit me. Bring him. He and I need to talk about how fast he rides that bike of his with you on it."

"You know I will. You're family, Greg. It would be my honor for you to meet Eugene and the kids."

"Kids, huh? Getting a pre-made family to boot? Well, good for you. It's about time someone made an honest woman out of you." If he only knew just how dishonest Eugene had really made me.

"They're going to need a grandpa figure in their life. Think you might want to be that for them?"

"Grandpa?" he considers it. "I like the sound of that. Bring the kids with you too."

"When do you go?"

"I'm on my way there now."

"Would you like a ride?"

"Nah," he answers with a dismissive wave. "They're supposed to send some van to collect me and my things. You let me get settled in for a couple of days and then come by."

Walking over, I hug him. He's stiff at first, but then he hugs me back. "Thank you for watching out for me." Releasing me, he backs away, shaking off the faintest look of sadness.

"Now don't go getting all emotional on me. I better get going before I miss the keepers from the VA coming to get me." Picking up my box, he hands it to me. "Don't forget your promise, or my burgers."

"I won't."

I watch him walk away before I let the tears flow freely. Knowing that he's going to be safe and looked after is the best last day of work gift I could have asked for. He's a good man who's had a hard life. It's high time he got to enjoy his golden years.

Unlocking the car door, I slide the box into the passenger seat. The top goes askew, and the edge of a file that I had tucked away into my personal effects peeks out.

The file containing my last act of helping someone in the system had failed. A system that's taken a year to even consider his right to access his birth records. Records that have been in our system since he was adopted from foster care at the age of two.

"Tyson Jackson, it's your lucky day."

I flip open the file, my phone at the ready to call him. While it rings, I finger out the copy I'd made of his birth certificate. My eyes scan the names as he picks up.

"Hello?"

All that escapes my lips is a gasp when I see the names listed.

## Judge

"MAKE A LEFT HERE," Grace says, pointing at a side street that's definitely not going to help us get to our destination.

"Put your finger down, woman," I tease. "I know where we're going."

"I have a stop to make first."

"A stop where?"

"Don't you worry about it. Just make a left. You'll see when we get there."

Natalie's head pokes up over the back of the seat. "Are we not going to see your friend? I thought that's where we were going."

"You and me both, kid," I grumble, but I follow Grace's directions, and once the coast is clear, I make a left.

She settles back in her seat, a smile plastered on her face, her hair blowing in the wind from the open window. She looks so different this way. No skinny skirts and tight buns. Instead, she wears ripped jeans, sandals, and a white shirt that shows off just the right amount of cleavage for my liking. And I like.

Her hair is loose, her lips are shiny with gloss, and if the kids weren't sitting in the backseat of this truck, I'd be pulling over to the side of the road to show my appreciation.

"We are," she assures us. "Greg's looking forward to meeting all of you."

"Is he like your grandpa or something?" Natalie asks.

Grace considers that. "Kinda," she replies. "More like a pseudo-uncle."

I look in the rearview mirror just in time to see Nat's nose crinkle in confusion. "A what uncle?"

"A pseudo-uncle," she repeats. "Like a pretend uncle. Or a stand-in uncle. He's not my real uncle, but he takes the place of one. That's why he wants to meet all of you. He said he wanted to meet my new family."

That word bounces around the inside of the truck with the weight of a bowling ball.

"We're your family?" Natalie questions, her eyes wide and filled with more hope than any thirteen-year-old girl should have to feel. And if I'm being honest, I'd like to hear the answer to that question too.

Smiling, she turns in her seat and reaches back, placing her hand on Natalie's knee. "Mr. Judge and I are in a new relationship," she tells her. "And I honestly can't make any promises on what will happen with that."

I frown, but wait for her to finish.

"But I know I love him very much. And I love you and Kevin very much too." She's never told me she loves me before. We're still so new, and everything has been so crazy. But she loves me. Those words hit me like a rocket, sending jolts of happiness through every single part of me.

But she's not done yet. "The four of us have been through more together than most biological families have been. No matter what happens between Mr. Judge and me, nothing will ever change that. We're a family. All four of us. That family will grow as we do, but there will always be the four of us, no matter what. Okay?"

Natalie swallows and nods, her eyes filled with tears.

"You okay with that, Kev?"

Kevin stares out the window. "Yeah, that's cool."

All I can see of him is the side of his cheek, and it's flushed a bright pink that's not usually there. Grace's words hit him as hard as they'd hit me.

"Oh, we're here! Turn into that coffee shop right

there." Grace's quiet, reassuring voice is gone, and now it's just plain excitement radiating off of her.

"What's going on, woman?" I ask, turning and searching for a place to park.

"You'll see."

Once I park the truck, she turns to me, her face bright and beaming. "I have a surprise for you. For all of you. Come on."

Her excitement is infectious, but I'm not a big fan of surprises. I get out of the truck, my mind whirling with all the different ideas on what sort of surprise could be waiting for us inside a coffee shop.

The kids and I follow her inside. Pausing, she looks around before making her way to a couch and loveseat set up with a coffee table between them.

I frown when I see the man sitting on the couch jump up as Grace approaches. I know this guy. It's Ty something or other. We'd shared a jail cell recently. But how the hell does he know Grace?

Ty has a young boy sitting on the couch beside him, his face covered in chocolate from the donut he's shoving into his mouth.

"Ms. Halfpenny," he greets with a nod, his gaze darting over to me with recognition. I relax a little at the formality. She obviously doesn't know this guy well if he doesn't even use her first name.

"Mr. Jackson," she returns, her voice suddenly all business. "Thank you for meeting me."

"Yeah," he replies, a little irritated. "I don't know why you wanted to, though. The judge still hasn't ruled on my case."

Grace moves and waves us closer, inviting us into their conversation. "Mr. Jackson, I'd like you to meet my boyfriend, Eugene Grant."

He looks as confused as I feel. "Hey," is all he says.

Kevin curls his lip and looks to me, clearly not understanding what the hell is going on, either.

"Okay, Grace, that's enough. What are we doing here?"

Grinning, she claps her hands together with excitement. "Okay, I'm sorry. I've never done anything like this before." She turns to Mr. Jackson. "I don't work for DFPS anymore. But, before you left, your file was on my desk and I took a peek at it." Jackson's brow smooths out, and the same hope I'd seen on Natalie's face earlier is on his now.

He glances down at his son, and then looks back to Grace. "Do you know who my parents are?"

She grabs my hand. "Tyson Jackson, I'd like you to meet your biological father, Eugene Grant."

Ty gapes at me as I gape at Grace. "What the fuck are you talking about, Grace?"

She places her hand on my chest. "Mr. Jackson has been petitioning the court to unseal his records. He was adopted when he was two years old, but his mother had surrendered him to DFPS as an infant."

I cross my arms, trying to keep my voice as calm as possible. "I don't have a son, Grace. My son died. He passed away before he was even two months old." I'd told her this. Why is she doing this?

But she isn't listening. "No, Eugene, she lied to you." *What did she just say?* I stare at her, unable to breathe. "Your son never died. She relinquished him, claiming that she couldn't care for him any longer. She gave him up to the state."

A punch in the dick would've hurt less than those words. My gaze slowly moves to the man standing in front of us. I take another long look at him. His eyes are dark, like mine. He's got several tattoos and a thin frame.

But it's the ears that do it for me.

I'd always hated my ears. Well, I'd always hated my earlobes, to be specific. They were longer than most, and thick. When I was younger, I used to keep my hair long just to cover them up. Since I started going gray, though, that just made me look like an old man.

I stare at him in shock and awe. Is it possible? Did Gina really give away our son and then lie to me about his death?

"So…" He clears his throat, looking as shocked as I feel. "So you're saying this is my father?" His hand is clutching at his chest as he stares back at me.

Grace reaches into her purse and pulls out a piece of yellowed paper and holds it in the air between us. "This is your birth certificate. The mother listed is Gina Marie Spicer." My heart thuds against my chest, feeling like the world has just… stopped. "And the father is Eugene Robert Grant." Her eyes meet mine. "Shane didn't die. She gave him away."

Feeling like I could pass out from the revelation, I drop my ass onto the loveseat and stare at the little boy across from me.

I clear my throat. "Who is this?" I ask, my voice hoarse with emotion.

"This is my son," Ty replies, his voice shaky. "His name is Joey."

My body trembles. Gina lied. I have a son. I have a grandson. I'm a fucking grandpa. How is any of this possible? I kissed my son on his forehead the night before I left, the last memory I had of him before Gina told me he'd died. Now, my boy has his own kid. My brain is on the brink of explosion.

I look at Grace, Natalie, and Kevin, barely able to wrap my head around how quickly things can change. Just a few months ago, I'd been a lonely man on the edge of fifty with nobody to come home to and only my club to rely on.

Now look at me. I have a woman, kids—a family for the first time in my life. The weight of it crashes down on me until the dam breaks under the incredible force of happiness I feel.

"Holy shit," I mumble, burying my face in my hands.

"Howy shit."

Lifting my head, I look at the toddler across from me. He's finished his donut, and now he's just grinning at me, knowing full well that the words he'd just repeated were ones he shouldn't have said, and not giving a single fuck.

"He really is your grandson," Kevin quips.

The laughter that erupts from my chest makes it hard to breathe. I don't even care, though. Oxygen doesn't matter right now. All the shit that had gone on in the past few days melts away, leaving only this little boy and me, and the fact that his father is the son I'd lost when I was only twenty years old.

As the others join in on my laughter, I look into Grace's eyes, knowing this is just the beginning. I've only known her a few short weeks, and already she's given me my family. *My son.* God, even thinking that word is strange to me. *My son* and I have a lot of catching up to do. A grandson. Kevin and Natalie are mine now. Hashtag saw to that with his paperwork. Everything that I wanted in my life is right here in front of me. Every fucking last thing.

All of that is enough to keep the joy of my laughter going, because I know that even after this moment, after the laughter has faded away, the joy I feel will stay with me. Now that we all have each other, the joy will stay with all of us.

I've found my home, and I'm never letting it go.

Epilogue

## Lindsey

Seeing him lying so still in that bed will haunt me until the day I die.

Karma has always been larger than life. An impenetrable force to be reckoned with. Always at the ready to tear down the world and kick some ass. But that's exactly why he's here in this bed, with so many tubes and wires coming out of him, isn't it? His need to protect me going too far over the edge, and now he could die and leave me forever. A forever I wasn't sure I wanted until this very moment. Leaving me alone. Stuck here with an empty space where our child once grew.

I'd never thought much about having children until after I had finished college and settled down, but those two little lines on that test changed it all for me. Since then, I'd planned for our future, and how we'd tell my uncle when the time was right. I'd thought about what that baby would look like, and who he or she would grow up to be. And now... now that baby will never be, and any future babies will never come along.

*We tried to save the baby. We tried to save your uterus, but the damage was too great.* The doctor's sorrowful words still haunt me.

Karma had so many hopes for the future, so many plans. When I'd told him about the pregnancy, and after we'd both gotten over the initial shock of it, he'd been over the moon.

From that moment on, he rarely left my side. He was my constant, gorgeous, yet annoyingly ever-present shadow. I couldn't get near anyone without seeing him right behind me, which made classes fun. No one expects to see a beast of a man like Karma sitting in on a chick lit class. But he went with me, rolling his eyes every single second until it ended. He loved our baby, and so did I. And then it was ripped away from us both in a blink of an eye. Our little miracle made from love, just... gone.

Its absence throbs in my numb and broken womb. A womb that will never carry life in it again thanks to that bastard, Henry Tucker. He gets to rot in prison while I lost my child, and Karma's life hangs in the balance, teetering on the scales of life and death. Henry deserved to die. Not my child, and not Karma.

How am I going to tell him about our baby? It'll break him even more. It'll break us. The last unbroken piece of my soul went with it. I have nothing left to cling to except for Karma. The last piece of my happiness.

The nurse adjusts the settings on Karma's IV line before finally leaving the room. I stare at him from the side of the bed, wanting nothing more than to have him wrap me up in his arms. I need him to tell me it's going to be okay. I just need him.

"You are the most amazing man," I whisper, unable to stop the tears from falling down my cheeks. "And I need you to get better. I can't do this without you, baby,"

A small crease appears between his brows. Can he hear me? That's impossible. He's got enough medication in his system to keep a grizzly bear down for a month. The sound of my voice may enter his ears, but he's high as a kite. He'd never understand what I'm saying.

The machines in the room whir and beep, helping to keep Karma's chest rising and falling with the help of a ventilator. It's all so dismal. Finally, I can't take it anymore. I gingerly move to the side of the bed and settle my ass on it, careful not to jostle either of us. Each movement I make is labored with my own still healing injuries, but I have to be here for him. I have to be the one who tells him what we lost that day, and I have to be close to him when I do.

Inside, my heart screams for him. Every fiber of my being begs for him to open his eyes. I need so bad for him to open those beautiful green emeralds I fell for the first time they turned my way. But it hasn't happened. He's been like this for nearly a week.

Leaning to the side, I turn my body, fitting myself onto the bed beside him. It isn't easy. There are monitors, cords, and wires everywhere, but nothing is going to deter me from placing my head on his shoulder when I say what I have to say.

Once settled, I place my hand on his belly and press a soft kiss to his furry cheek. "I love you so much," I whisper. "And I'm so sorry."

A sob rips through me, and even though I'd just taken my pain medication, it does little to numb the physical pain the sob causes.

"I'm so sorry, baby. I'm so fucking sorry." Tears slide down my cheeks, dotting the white linen underneath our clutched hands. I give it a squeeze, hoping he returns it, but he doesn't. And I still don't know if he ever will again.

---

Read more about Karma's story in Dark Desires.

The Series

Dark Protector

Dark Secret

Dark Guardian

Dark Desires

Dark Destiny

Dark Redemption

Dark Salvation

Dark Seduction

Avelyn Paige is a USA Today and Wall Street Journal bestselling author who writes stories about dirty alpha males and the brave women who love them. She resides in a small town in Indiana with her husband and three fuzzy kids, Jezebel, Cleo, and Asa.

Avelyn spends her days working as a cancer research scientist and her nights sipping moonshine while writing. You can often find her curled up with a good book surrounded by her pets or watching one of her favorite superhero movies for the billionth time. Deadpool is currently her favorite.

Also by Avelyn Paige

The Heaven's Rejects MC Series

Heaven Sent

Angels and Ashes

Sins of the Father

Absolution

Lies and Illusions

The Dirty Bitches MC Series

Dirty Bitches MC #1

Dirty Bitches MC #2

Dirty Bitches MC #3

Other Books by Avelyn Paige

Girl in a Country Song

Cassie's Court

Geri Glenn writes alpha males. She is a USA Today Bestselling Author, best known for writing motorcycle romance, including the Kings of Korruption MC series. She lives in the Thousand Islands with her two young girls, one big dog and one terrier that thinks he's a Doberman,, a hamster and two guinea pigs whose names she can never remember.

Before she began writing contemporary romance, Geri worked at several different occupations. She's been a pharmacy assistant, a 911 dispatcher, and a caregiver in a nursing home. She can say without a doubt though, that her favorite job is the one she does now—writing romance that leaves an impact.

# Also By Geri Glenn

## The Kings of Korruption MC series.

Ryker

Tease

Daniel

Jase

Reaper

Bosco

## Korrupted Novellas:

Corrupted Angels

Reinventing Holly

## Other Books by Geri Glenn

Dirty Deeds (Satan's Wrath MC)

Hood Rat

Printed in Great Britain
by Amazon

19533310R00149